Pamela Fudge works as a part-time administrator at Bournemouth University and has written poetry since she was a child. She started writing fiction in 1983 and has had short stories published in most of the national women's magazines in the country. Her previous books include *Second Best*, *High Infidelity* and *A Blessing in Disguise*.

You can find out more about her at: www.pamfudge.co.uk.

# A CHANGE FOR THE BETTER

Jo Farrell has spent her whole life caring for others, but with the timely departure of both her alcoholic husband and her demanding mother, Jo finally has the peaceful existence she's always craved. Finally, she has a chance to look at herself . . . but when she does, she doesn't much like what she sees. Jo has no idea where to start so she makes a list of all the things she once planned to do before life got the better of her . . . and as she starts to make changes, her life comes together in ways she never expected . . .

*Books by Pamela Fudge*
*Published by The House of Ulverscroft:*

RELUCTANT FOR ROMANCE
ROMANTIC MELODY
WIDOW OF THE WORLD
HIGH INFIDELITY
A BLESSING IN DISGUISE
SECOND BEST

PAMELA FUDGE

# A CHANGE FOR THE BETTER

*Complete and Unabridged*

# ULVERSCROFT
Leicester

First published in Great Britain in 2010 by
Robert Hale Limited
London

First Large Print Edition
published 2011
by arrangement with
Robert Hale Limited
London

British Library CIP Data

Fudge, Pamela, *1946 –*
    A change for the better.
    1. Single women- -Fiction.
    2. Life change events- -Fiction.
    3. Large type books.
    I. Title
    823.9′2–dc22

    ISBN 978–1–4448–0816–2

Published by
F. A. Thorpe (Publishing)
Anstey, Leicestershire

Set by Words & Graphics Ltd.
Anstey, Leicestershire
Printed and bound in Great Britain by
T. J. International Ltd., Padstow, Cornwall

This book is printed on acid-free paper

In loving memory of my Mum and Dad
who encouraged my love of
reading and writing

This book is for you both with my love

# Acknowledgements

My gratitude, as always, goes to all at Robert Hale Ltd, especially John Hale for liking *A Change For The Better* enough to publish it, Nikki Edwards, Gill Jackson, Nick Chaytor, Catherine Williams and David Young, who make the process from manuscript through to a beautifully produced book such a seamless process.

Many thanks to Dee Steed at Waterstones Poole branch, who offered me my first book signing opportunity several years ago and a book launch for every newly published novel since. Also to Miss Davies, the English tutor who told me I should be writing stories when I was about twelve years old, and to Jean Dynes, the writing tutor who set me on the road to becoming a published author many years later.

I am blessed with the best family in the world, and the best friends, who love and support me in everything I do — attending every book launch, purchasing every novel and giving me the very best reviews — fellow writers, such as Pam W, Chris H, Nora, Lyndsay, Alan, Bruna, Ann, Rob R, Cass and

Janie, those I work with within the Admissions Office at Bournemouth University, such as Pam M, Kate H, Sarah, Kate T, Jill, Jane, Gail, Angela, Alison, Katrina and the brilliant midwifery team, those I relax with, including Karen, Chris N, Jan, Nicky, Sally, Robert M and Robert B and many more.

My love and thanks go to my sisters, my stepchildren and my gorgeous grandchildren, also to my web-master and stepson, Mark, and his family.

Most of all, I would like to thank my children, as always, Shane, Kelly, Scott and not forgetting Mike and Jess.

Your belief in me gives me self-belief. I couldn't do it without you all.

# 1

The supermarket was heaving. All around me people were chattering and laughing as they picked up popcorn and pizzas, all set for a Friday night of family entertainment in front of a suitable DVD. I listened to them debating the qualities of ham and pineapple topping versus pepperoni and tried not to be envious. It wasn't easy.

All I had to get excited about was a solo viewing of Emmerdale, followed by Coronation Street, Eastenders, and a frozen chicken dinner for one. I stared at the packet with its appetizing illustration as if it was somehow going to manifest itself into a family-size lasagne — complete with the family — and wondered what had happened to that woman who had once actually looked forward to eating in peace with only the TV for company. Quite shocking to realize just how bad things must have seemed at one time in my life for the option to have been so appealing to me.

Well — I dropped the frozen dinner into the wire basket without enthusiasm — I'd finally got the quiet life I'd always craved. It was amazing how quickly a peaceful existence had begun to pall, until I'd reached the stage when I wanted something — anything — to happen to liven things up.

Another Friday night, another empty weekend stretching ahead of me, and I wondered if this really was all there was to life for a woman of my age.

A frozen jam roly-poly and custard joined the chicken dinner, together with a paperback I'd seen recommended in the book section of the local paper, a celebrity magazine and a packet of walnut whips. As an afterthought, I picked up a bunch of yellow chrysanthemums in an effort to brighten what was rapidly becoming a very glum mood.

'Doing anything nice at the weekend, Jo?' The girl on the checkout sounded interested, but she wasn't even looking at me as she scanned the goods and, at my request, popped everything into one of the Cheapsmart 'green' reusable bags.

I thought she might be new, since her name escaped me, though she obviously recognized me, probably from my role in the Human Resources department of this local branch of the supermarket chain we both worked for.

I'd have thought the items in my basket would have given my weekend plans away but I doubt she'd even noticed what they were, never mind what they signified.

'Oh, you know,' I said drily, dutifully retrieving remnants of my sense of humour from somewhere, 'a couple of sherberts at my local tonight, boogying the night away at Sam's Night Spot until late on Saturday, prior to flying off to Paris for Sunday lunch with Richard Gere.'

She did look at me then — as if I was quite mad — but then it dawned on her that I was joking and she laughed politely. Obviously, the very thought that a woman over fifty could have any sort of life outside of work had never really occurred to her — and why would it when it had never really occurred to me?

I wandered aimlessly along the street, carrier bag swinging from one hand, looking into shop windows and wondering at the reflection of the tired old woman trudging along that I barely recognized as me.

I'd always had boundless energy and, by God, I had needed it in my time. Life with an alcoholic husband had been no picnic, and you only had to add to that a demanding hypochondriac mother and a tearaway son and you pretty much had the picture, but I was a fighter — always had been — until now when it seemed I finally had nothing left to fight for.

At home I worked my way steadily, though unenthusiastically, through the microwaved dinner, the dessert quickly followed, and the three walnut whips one after the other. It was only when the food was all gone that I realized I hadn't tasted a single thing. Apart from the soaps, there was nothing on the TV, the book didn't grab me as it should have done and I flicked open the magazine in a desultory fashion. Two or three pages of looking at pretty young things wearing next to nothing and hanging on the arm of the current 'squeeze' — whatever *that* was when it was at home — and I threw the glamorous publication across the room in exasperation.

I passed it lying on the floor when I went to make yet another cup of tea and it was the sight of Helen Mirren staring up at me from the glossy pages that brought me up short.

Now, there was a woman who knew what she wanted and had found the determination from somewhere to go out there and get it. She had to be about my age, probably even older, but showed no sign of retiring — though she surely could easily have afforded to — and she also carried her mature years with ease. She was obviously a woman comfortable in her own body and definitely her own person. How I envied her.

When the phone rang five minutes later I

hadn't moved an inch, but was still standing there, deep in thought, staring down at the smiling face of the sort of woman I could never hope to be.

I hurried to pick up in case it was Petie. 'Hello.'

'Hi, Mum, how y'doing?'

Those few words were all it took to lift my mood and I felt a smile curve the corners of my mouth. 'I'm *fine*,' I replied with great emphasis, not wanting to be one of those mothers who burdened her child with all the minutiae of day-to-day living. I'd had more than enough of that from my own, God rest her complaining soul.

'That's great to hear,' Petie sounded really pleased, and I marvelled again at how much the former tearaway had changed. 'Got something nice planned for the weekend?'

My heart sank and I realized, too late, that without admitting it even to myself I had kept the hope in the back of my mind that he would be paying one of his flying visits. 'Oh, but I was hoping . . . weren't you going to try . . . ?'

'Not going to be able to make it even for lunch on Sunday, I'm afraid.' He did sound sorry, but as he went on his young voice was full of enthusiasm. 'Since Adam acquired Siddons' Construction we've got work coming out of our ears. You wouldn't believe how well we're doing.'

I thought I would, since I worked with Adam's wife, Denise, who talked about little else. I had to be pleased, and grateful, too, because what was good for the company was good for Petie.

It had been Adam who had given my son the chance that no other employer would with his unfortunate criminal record, and that had been the making of him. However, after battling so long to keep him on the straight and narrow, I suddenly found myself surplus to requirements and that hurt a bit. Well, it hurt a lot actually. No one likes to feel useless.

'Oh, I can imagine,' I agreed with an enthusiasm I didn't feel, 'but don't worry, I have more than enough to do to occupy my time.'

'Good old Mum,' I could hear Petie smiling, 'time for yourself now you've finally got your errant son off your hands, eh? And you so deserve it. You believed in me when no one else did, bailed me out, patched me up and sorted me out, time and time and time again. How come you never, ever, gave up on me? No one would have blamed you if you had, you know.'

'You're my boy,' I said simply. 'Giving up

on you wouldn't have changed that and I just felt that if I held on in there, eventually, you would either change for the better or come to a sticky end. I kept praying it would be the former, and now I couldn't be more proud of you.'

'You're a mum in a million, you are. All those words of wisdom finally went home, but it took a while, didn't it? Thanks, Mum. I love you.'

Petie said it often these days, but it still never failed to bring a tear to my eye. Probably because I never thought I would see the day. I was sure there were times when he'd hated me. I was damn sure there were times I hated him — but never quite enough to give up on him.

'I love you, too, and I'm proud of you.'

'About time too, eh? How many times did you say, 'If you're not happy with your life, Petie, what are *you* going to do about it, because *you're* the only one who can change it.' You know what, Mum?'

'What's that, love?' I encouraged, intrigued to hear what was coming next.

'You were right,' he said and then he was gone and I was left staring at the telephone receiver burring in my hand and with my own oft-quoted words ringing in my ears.

The phone was returned to its stand with

the familiar bleep and for a minute or two I was mesmerized by the red light and regretted I couldn't also be plugged in and recharged. Then I went back to the magazine and studied the example of living life to the full as set by an award-winning actress.

She could easily have said, as a great many actresses of a certain age do and with annoying regularity, that there were no decent film parts for women over forty and simply retired gracefully. She could have gone the other route and resorted to the surgeon's knife in an effort to recapture her youth and compete for younger roles.

What she had done was act not only her age but everyone else off the large or small screen until, finally, she had received the recognition she deserved. What she hadn't done was to give up and there had to be a lesson for me there, somewhere.

I'd never be a Helen Mirren, and I probably wouldn't even want to be. Each to our own, after all, and my acting skills had always left a lot to be desired. I cringed every time I thought about my Juliet in the school play — it had been a serious case of miscasting — and I was still rubbish at charades.

The actress was simply an example of what could be achieved if you put your mind to it and there were many others like her, in all walks of life. You didn't need to be rich and famous to be happy. The words 'If you're not happy with your life, what are *you* going to do about it, because *you're* the only one who can change it' were the sharp reminder I needed to stop feeling sorry for myself and *do something*.

# 2

An hour had gone by since Petie's phone call and I was making a list — or trying to. In truth, all I had succeeded in doing was to chew the blue end off the cheap ballpoint pen I was using and get ink that took a lot of removing all over my teeth and lips. I just didn't have a clue where to start.

It had been years since I had given a thought to anything more than getting the rent paid and keeping food on the table and yet once, a very long time ago, I'd had such plans for my life.

I'd made an excellent start by making sure I left school with enough qualifications and suitable office skills under my belt to land a decent job earning a decent wage. The middle child from a working-class family, I'd been determined to better myself and was already headed in the right direction when I met Jack Farrell and headed straight to the hell of marriage to an alcoholic instead.

He was older, good-looking in a Sean Connery sort of way, very charming — and a heavy drinker, just like my own father. You'd have thought I'd have recognized the signs and taken to my heels but, as I've already said, he was a charmer. He told me I was his soulmate, but almost as soon as we were married it became clear I was simply his meal ticket. By then my self-esteem was so low I didn't have the confidence required simply to up and leave.

Anyway, he was gone now — no doubt to a better place — and I didn't miss him — or the mother who had moved in and taken over chipping away at my confidence where he left off. The only thing I had to thank Jack for was Petie — and I did, every day of my life, because even when Petie was at his worst and getting into every scrape imaginable I wouldn't have been without him. I couldn't be more proud that he had finally turned his life around.

Which brought me right back to how I was going to manage to do the same with mine because, as I'd just been made fully aware, it was entirely down to me. What were those amazing plans I'd once had for my life? The plans that went out of the window the minute Jack Farrell came in through the door.

Looking back, it seemed ridiculous that I had allowed him to turn my head when the qualifications necessary for a better future had been gained in spite of my parents' constant 'encouragement' to 'go out there

11

and get a bloody job'. I'd compromised by staying on at school and getting a weekend job so that I could contribute my share to the family coffers, then going to college in the evenings and working during the day to further my education.

The desire to better myself made me an outsider in my own family, accused of being a 'snob' and a 'swot' by my nearest and dearest. I suppose it was no wonder I had seen Jack as a form of escape. He'd looked so handsome and prosperous in the sharp suits he wore as a double-glazing salesman, and his plans for the future had more than matched my own.

He was, 'going places,' he assured me. If only I had known the only place he was going on a regular basis was the nearest pub, that the salesman's job was only the last in a very long line of the job titles on his employment record and that everyone at the job centre knew him by name, I might have had an indication of what I was letting myself in for.

I shrugged dismissively; that was then and those times were over. At least over the years I'd always had a decent job, and that had given me the means to keep a roof over our heads, even if there was little time or energy left to give a thought to any of the other plans I might have had.

Still, there was no point in looking

backwards. I poised the pen again, determined to make a start, and then almost jumped out of my skin when the doorbell rang. I automatically looked at the clock and wondered who on earth would be calling at past nine o'clock at night.

Expecting to see the Avon lady or someone collecting for charity, I was surprised, instead, to find my scruffy downstairs neighbour on the step. He wore his usual attire of a cheap tracksuit — so unsuitable for a man of his age, well, any age really — and shabby trainers. His grey hair looked as if it could do with a good wash and cut, though even showing it a brush would have improved the state of it no end. I prevented my lip curling in disgust only with great difficulty.

'Mr Masters.' I knew my tone was abrupt to the point of rudeness, but I didn't particularly care. He wasn't my favourite person at any time of the day and at nine in the evening he was the very last person I wanted to see. 'What can I do for you?'

He shuffled uncomfortably in his ill-fitting shoes. 'I wondered if you'd received your copy of the *Advertiser*,' he said in the cultured tones that always took me by surprise. Sounding almost urgent and as if the delivery of the local 'freebie' newspaper was of immense importance to him, he continued, 'only they seem to have bypassed me and there's an article in there I particularly want to read.'

I frowned, and cursing the good manners that insisted I remained civil, I said, 'I'm not sure. Sometimes it doesn't get delivered until Saturday, but I'll just see if it was in the pile of stuff I picked up off the mat when I came in.'

I turned around, and to my surprise and dismay he followed me inside. Usually he was very aloof. It was as much as he could ever do to muster a greeting when we passed on the stairs of the three-storey building, and then it was often in the form of a complaint about something or other.

I bit back a sarcastic 'Come in, why don't you?' and concentrated instead on finding the publication he was after, so that I could get rid of him sooner rather than later.

'Ah,' I pounced on the newspaper triumphantly and pushed it into his hands, ignoring the various glossy leaflets advertising anything from furniture to food that slid from between the pages and onto the floor.

He stared down at the paper, his thinning hair drooping into his eyes, and without looking back up, he said, 'I'll bring it back as soon as I've finished with it.'

'Oh, don't bother, I rarely bother to read it.

I prefer a good book myself.' Then I had a thought and hesitated, unwilling to give him an excuse to return, but suddenly tempted by the opportunities for betterment that might lie within the printed sheets. I was well aware that if I waited another week, I might never get started.

'Yes?' Obviously sensing my uncertainty, he did look up then.

'Actually, I will have it back when you've done with it,' I nodded, and then found myself adding an explanation that clearly wasn't expected or needed, 'I've been thinking of taking a course or something.'

'I'd have thought you had quite enough to do,' he said, frowning, 'you already work full-time, don't you?'

I took it as a criticism and practically jumped down his throat. 'I am entitled to a life outside of work, you know, and anyway, it's none of your damn business what I do.'

He stepped back away from my fury, and I thought he would leave immediately. I'm not sure which of us was more surprised when he did no such thing, but laughed apologetically and agreed, 'You're right, of course, on both counts. I'm afraid living on my own for so long has made me far too opinionated, simply because there's no one to disagree with me. I'm surprised by how refreshing I find it when someone does. Was there any particular course you had in mind? Just out of neighbourly interest, you understand.'

I had no idea how it happened, but he was the first person who'd shown any interest in my life for a very long time and suddenly I found myself telling him all about my plans to better myself, plans that would require quite a bit of dusting off because they had been on hold for so long, if and when I remembered what they might have been.

An hour later he was still there, by which time we had shared a pot of tea and a list was beginning to take shape, numbered and in no particular order.

1. Learn to drive (Greg — that was his name, I'd discovered — insisted I wasn't too old and I'd recalled it was one of the things that had been on my original list all those years ago).

'I could teach you,' he'd offered, but when I got over my amazement I refused as nicely as I could. A leopard never changes its spots and I could think of nothing worse than spending an hour at a time in the confines of a car taking tuition from a grumpy and none too clean old man.

2. Learn to sew (At least he couldn't offer to teach me that and I'd always quite liked the idea of being able to run up a stunning creation from a few scraps of material and a packet of sequins).
3. Learn to decorate cakes (I used to make a mean fruit cake, if I said so myself, though there seemed little point now that Petie wasn't around so much to appreciate them. It might be nice to decorate a cake for Christmas, however, and I'd always envied people who could).
4. Update my image (Greg gave me a bit of a sideways look at this one, as well he might since his own image could obviously do with a radical overhaul).

Though he didn't comment I found myself explaining that I was sick of the person I saw looking back at me everyday in the mirror and how I'd seen the amazing things they did with a bit of make-up and a new hairstyle on these make-over shows on the TV.

5. Learn to do something artistic, like writing poetry or painting water colours (A bit of a tall order, since I was well aware I didn't have an artistic bone in my body, but what the hell! I could try,

couldn't I? This last was directed at Greg who wisely said little apart from murmuring encouragingly).

6. Holiday abroad (I had never even holidayed in this country, but living a stone's throw from Bournemouth and relatively close to the New Forest meant Petie got his share of trips to the seaside and countryside when he was growing up. I could have settled for a nice holiday in the UK, but this was a grown-up list, and I felt I wanted to spread my wings, literally, and fly somewhere exotic).

'I can't believe you've never flown,' Greg said, with the stunned reaction of someone who had obviously travelled the world in his time.

'No money, no time, and no real desire,' I replied briefly, 'but I would like to be able to say I'd been abroad at least once. A matter of pride, you might say, since I work with people who think nothing of hopping on a plane at a moment's notice.'

7. Diet (My look dared Greg to offer any comment at all. Whatever he said would probably have encouraged a violent reaction. If he'd politely said there was

no need I'd have called him a liar to his face, and if he'd said I should diet I'd have said it was a case of the pot calling the kettle black and that it certainly wouldn't do him any harm to lose a few pounds).

8. Move house or at least decorate (This was a biggy, but it had been on my mind for years. This was the home I had once shared with Jack and although eventually there had been Petie, too, there had also been my mother and it was in this flat that I had spent some of my unhappiest times. Even changing the appearance of the place would be cleansing, I thought).

I didn't go into any of this with Greg. Very few people knew anything about my life with an alcoholic husband and that was the way I wanted it to stay. I'd lived in the building longer than any of the residents of this or any of the neighbouring blocks of flats and I had managed to shed my past. My respectable widowed status was now accepted without question or comment.

9. Get my ears pierced (This was something I had wanted since I was a school girl — along with a tattoo. My

enthusiasm for a tattoo had waned but I still longed to be able to wear pretty earrings that didn't pinch my earlobes so badly that the jewellery always ended up in my handbag).

10. To visit a clairvoyant (Greg's eyebrows disappeared up into his receding hairline at this, but I ignored him. This was my list — not his — and I would damn well put anything on it that took my fancy).

'Ten.' I sat back, very well pleased with the progress made since Greg had joined me. 'I think that will be enough to be going on with, don't you?'

He might have had his reservations about some of the items on the list but, to his credit, he simply asked mildly, 'What will you do, start at the top and work your way from one through to ten?'

I laughed in disbelief at his naivety. 'You don't really expect me to do them all, do you? It's taken me about thirty years just to write the list.'

'So what if it takes you the next thirty to accomplish them all, it would be good to at least try, wouldn't it? Think about it.'

He rose then to take his leave, and I found I was almost sorry to see him go. I shrugged as I closed the door behind him, accepting that I must be getting soft in my old age. I didn't even *like* him, for heaven's sake.

I cleared away the tea things and noticed the *Advertiser* on the floor by the side of the sofa Greg had been sitting on. The article couldn't have been that important, then, but I would pop it through his door in the morning all the same. It had been quite nice to have a bit of company for once, even his, but I still wasn't in a hurry to repeat the experience.

★　★　★

'Was that Mr Masters I saw coming out of your place last night?'

I stifled a groan. I'd walked right into that, hadn't I? Served me right for coming straight out of my front door without checking the coast was clear first.

Miss Gutheridge — her name was Edna, though no one ever called her anything but Miss Gutheridge — was planted firmly in my way, dark eyes burning with an inquisitiveness that was more than friendly interest. The yellow duster that gave her the excuse, if she needed one, to be positioned on the landing at all hours of the day or night, and seemed permanently attached to her hand, actually trembled with her barely suppressed excitement.

21

I supposed I should feel sorry for the neighbour who shared my landing. She was obviously very lonely, but as she was also very, very nosy, the annoyance at the one thing kind of cancelled out the sympathy for the other. I must have hesitated just that little bit too long because she jumped in with a prompt.

'I wouldn't have thought he was at all your cup of tea.'

'He came up to borrow my *Advertiser*,' I said acidly, annoyed for feeling under pressure to explain something that was none of her damn business, then realizing, too late, I was holding that very newspaper in my hand and she was looking from it to me in clear disbelief. 'We got talking and he forgot to take it with him,' I continued, furious with myself for imparting even more information, but carrying on just the same, 'I'm just on my way to pop it through his door, so if you'll excuse me.'

I almost had to push my way past her and knew she would go straight back to 'polishing her letterbox', so that she could overhear any exchange there might be between myself and Greg on the next landing down.

He was standing at his front door wearing the same clothes as he'd had on the night before when I got there, and must have heard

22

the whole thing because he put a finger to his lips, and then pointed upwards. Rapping his own doorknocker, he made a great pretence of opening the door to me.

'My dear Mrs Farrell,' he said loudly so there was no chance of Edna missing a word, 'How very kind of you to bring the newspaper down to me. Do come inside, as I would value your opinion on a particular item included in the article I told you about.'

Before I could demur, I was ushered inside and the door was closed behind me with a very definite slam.

Opening my mouth to ask Greg just what the hell he thought he was playing at, I found him leaning against the door, his shoulders shaking with evident mirth. It only took a second or two before my own lips began to curl.

'You,' I said, 'are very naughty. She'll put two and two together and have us married off by Christmas.'

'I've always wanted to give her something to really talk about,' he smiled, looking pleased, and then added, 'and you can put her straight tomorrow. Now come on through and I'll put the kettle on. The gleam on that letterbox will be enough to blind you by the time you go back up.'

He had a sense of humour, then. Who

would have thought it? I'd seen no indication of a lighter side to his rather morose nature in all the time we had lived in the same building. I was also pleasantly surprised by how neat and clean his flat was. I suppose I had been expecting it to be as shabby and unkempt as he was. The layout mirrored my own home but, unlike mine, with its piles of books and magazines waiting to be read, Greg obviously had a place for everything and everything was kept in its place. I was impressed in spite of myself.

'Seeing how light and airy your place is makes me want to start number eight on the list right away,' I told him as I hovered in the kitchen doorway and watched him arranging cups and saucers on a tray.

'Moving house or decorating?' he asked, adding with a little smile, 'I hope it's not the former, or Miss Gutheridge will swear I've driven you away.'

'The idea of moving does appeal,' I admitted, 'but the huge upheaval and expense of actually doing it doesn't. Is that cake homemade?' I gasped as Greg lifted a Victoria sponge out of the cupboard. 'You're making me feel very lax. I can't even recall the last time I made a cake, though I used to enjoy baking.'

'But you work full-time,' he reminded me,

as if that explained everything, 'and I don't work at all. I have to fill the hours somehow. The trouble is I also end up eating the results so you would be helping me out if you would enjoy at least one slice.' He lifted the tray and walked past me into the living room, urging me to, 'sit down, sit down, please'.

I don't know what we talked about, everything and nothing at all really, but before I knew it an hour had flown by and when I realized I stood up quickly, reminding him that my reputation would be in tatters.

Seeing the concerned look on Greg's face, I simply smiled mischievously and said, 'Well, it's a very long time since anyone can have found anything interesting to say about me, either, so it actually makes a nice change, but now I really must go.'

'Going somewhere nice?' he asked and then, before I could reply, he put a hand up and said firmly, 'No, forget I even asked that, it's none of my business. One nosy old biddy in the block is quite enough.'

I laughed, and told him, 'It's hardly a secret. I was popping into town, but now I think I might have a look round B and Q to get some ideas for my redecorating scheme. Mind you, working up the enthusiasm to start might take a bit more effort on my part.'

'Would you like some company?' Greg

sounded almost eager. 'I could give you a lift. You don't drive, do you? Sorry, stupid question, since learning was number one on your list.'

I hadn't expected him to offer and didn't quite know how to refuse. I could hardly tell him I wouldn't be seen dead walking round the local DIY store with him looking like that. Even I had my standards.

'And make Miss Gutheridge's day.' I made a joke out of my refusal and tried not to notice the disappointment in Greg's surprisingly blue eyes. 'Thanks, anyway, but I think we've given her enough to talk about for now.'

I knew I had made the right decision, but I still had cause to regret it when I saw the vast array of paints and paper on display in the huge store and realized I hadn't a clue what I was looking for. It might have helped if I even had some idea where I was going to start.

After wandering up and down the aisles, getting more and more confused, I followed the smell of fresh coffee and was soon sitting down with a steaming cup in front of me, and a fresh doughnut. I managed to retrieve an old receipt from the depths of my handbag and a stub of pencil.

The list wasn't very long. There were only six rooms — all of them fairly compact

— and a hallway in the flat, but I listed them carefully anyway.

1. Sitting room
2. Kitchen
3. My bedroom
4. Spare bedroom
5. Boxroom
6. Toilet/bathroom combined
7. Hallway

The sensible side of me knew I should start somewhere like the spare bedroom or even the tiny boxroom. Somewhere my amateur efforts wouldn't notice too much if it all went wrong, but a newly discovered reckless side of me wanted to start somewhere that would make a real difference.

I thought about the woodchip paper in the hallway, emulsioned a lemon shade years ago by Jack in one of his more sober moments. It might have looked attractive once but now it just looked shabby. I did remember someone telling me once it would be an absolute nightmare to get woodchip off the walls and I quailed at the thought of all that scraping.

However, once I'd made the decision simply to paint over it there was no stopping me, and I refused to be nonplussed by the colour choice. I'd already made my mind up I didn't want magnolia, thinking it a particularly insipid shade, but the rich cream I eventually decided on came in so many variations that I almost gave up and went home. In desperation, I moved on to the white paint I fancied for the woodwork, and that was nearly as bad.

I was agonizing over gloss, silk or matt, one coat or non-drip and the various makes and prices, when a familiar voice full of surprise said, 'Mum? What on earth are you doing here? I just left your place and even Miss Gutheridge didn't have a clue where you were, though she seemed to know exactly what you've been up to. She wasted no time at all telling me about the new man in your life. I must say, you're a bit of a dark horse.'

# 3

'OK, Mum, OK,' Petie pleaded, taking a step back and staring at me in astonishment — as well he might, since I very much doubted he had seen me fly off the handle like that in his entire twenty-six years of life. Added to that, I couldn't have chosen a more public place to do it if I had tried.

'Is this young man bothering you?' a quite elderly store assistant asked me in a worried tone, obviously concerned at having to intervene but feeling obliged to do so all the same.

I dragged a weak smile from somewhere. 'No more than usual.' The touch of humour was forced. 'He's my son.'

'Oh, I see,' the man said, and I thought he probably did. He had the look of a family man. He certainly had plenty of the wrinkles that generally characterize parents with plenty of mileage under their belt. He was clearly relieved to receive a request from another customer looking for brass screws and shot away as fast as his bowlegs could carry him.

'I wasn't having a go,' Petie said cautiously, running a distracted hand through his floppy fair hair and setting his glasses straight on his nose before adding, 'in fact, I was really pleased for you if it's true. You're entitled to a life, you know, and a love life.'

I huffed furiously and frowned up at him, 'I don't need my own son to tell me that, Petie. I've actually already made the decision to make some changes in my life and to my home, which is what brings me here. As for a love life, only I will decide if and when I want such a thing — and I only I will decide who that might be with. I certainly don't need some nosy old bag to invent one for me.'

I couldn't believe I was so angry, but what had seemed like fun when I was sharing the humour of winding up Miss Gutheridge with Greg now seemed far from funny. If she was tattling about this non-existent romance to Petie, who else was she sharing the juicy details with?

'She's just lonely, Mum,' Petie excused, reminding me of something I already knew and should have allowed for before judging her. 'She doesn't really mean any harm. I'm sure she'd be delighted if you and this Masters guy really were an item. Who is he, anyway? Do I know him?'

'No, I don't think so. He moved into his flat downstairs after you moved out of ours, though you might have seen him on the stairs.' I wrinkled my nose. 'He's kind of scruffy.'

'Yeah, that's what Edna said,' Petie grinned, 'but she also said he was loaded.'

'Now where on earth can she have got that from? He'd hardly be living where he is if he was rich, would he?' I shook my head. 'Honestly, what that woman can't find out she just makes right up. If she had a brain she'd be dangerous, I can tell you.'

Finally, we both laughed, and I reached out to touch Petie's arm, 'I'm sorry I shouted at you like that — especially in the middle of B and Q. What are you doing here, anyway?'

'My drill burned out and Adam said to pop along here and pick one up. The local builders' merchants are all closed for the weekend now and we're going to need it first thing in the morning.'

'If you're working Sundays, too, Adam must have a lot on, but you should get a break, you know.'

'I don't mind. It's a rush job. I'm getting paid overtime, and a few days off when it's done, too. He's a great boss.'

I nodded. We both appreciated what an understatement that was because I couldn't think of anyone else in the world who'd have been willing to take a chance on Petie.

I liked to think that Petie had more than

repaid Adam's belief that there was more to my son than the exploits that had almost landed him with the prison sentence even I recognized he would have richly deserved.

'And you're a great Mum,' Petie hugged me, 'the very best. Now, what was it you were looking for?'

★　★　★

Funny how what had been so confusing became so simple the minute I was being guided by someone who knew exactly what he was doing. In no time, Petie had nipped off to collect the trolley I hadn't even given a thought to. Ridiculous really, as just two tins of paint would have filled the orange basket I held and then how had I been going to carry the rest of my purchases?

He agreed with me that painting over the shabby woodchip would be the quickest and easiest way to make a change. 'I would come round and strip the lot off for you,' he said, 'but you would have to wait for a while — and I don't think you want to hang around now that you've decided to make a start.'

'No time like the present,' I said with a confidence that I was far from feeling.

I felt even less confident when Petie had dropped me back home and helped me upstairs with my purchases. Faced with the materials and tools piled up in my own hallway, I was quite certain I must have been completely mad even to dream I could tackle such a mammoth task. I'd never painted so much as a picture before, never mind a whole wall. To say the prospect of starting was daunting was a massive understatement, but leaving everything sitting there unused was not an option. What was I — a woman or a wimp?

I covered the carpet with the dustsheets Petie had insisted I buy, despite my protesting, 'But it says the paint is non-drip. Look.' He'd just given me a look, shook his head, and put the sheets in the trolley anyway.

I was well aware a real makeover would have involved not only stripping the walls but also replacing the carpet with new. The carpet had been down for years and was a bit faded and worn in places, but replacing it would mean an additional expense I was reluctant to contemplate. I wasn't exactly broke, but neither was I rich, and a lifetime of struggling to make ends meet had given me a very real fear of finding myself with nothing in the pot for when the inevitable rainy day arrived.

A new carpet, I decided firmly, would just have to wait. I braced myself to make a start on the ceiling, because even I, with no idea at all of the correct procedures, managed to work out that you must start at the top and work down.

I swiftly discovered that (a) one coat emulsion on a very discoloured ceiling was going to take at least two and (b) non-drip paint wasn't. I was still delighted with the speed I managed to roller the paint across the ceiling and was less than bothered by the dollops of white that landed on my clothes and hair. Before I put the lid back on the tub I'd already decided the second coat would go on first thing the following morning and that I might even make a start on the walls after that.

I wasn't expecting the telephone to ring and to my chagrin managed to get paint all over the receiver trying to pick it up. I thought I very probably had it all over my ear, too, and tried not to think about it.

'I thought we'd have lunch here instead of going out tomorrow,' Denise said without preamble, knowing she needed no introduction, being not only my immediate boss at work, but a very dear friend, too.

Widowed while she was only in her forties, she was now remarried to her late husband's best friend, Adam, who was also Petie's boss.

Much as I loved her, my heart sank. I'd

forgotten about accepting the invitation to lunch anyway and going along was going to scupper my decorating plans for the following day. Also the fact Denise was planning a meal at home could only mean one thing — she had a man lined up for me to meet.

So happy to have found love again herself, Denise seemed to have made it her mission in life to find a special someone for me, and all my protestations that I was happy as I was washed right over her.

She must have noticed my hesitation and asked, 'You haven't forgotten, have you? We were only talking about it yesterday.'

'Of course not,' I lied stoutly, crossing my paint-spattered fingers, 'I'm looking forward to it.'

'Good, that's settled then. Adam has promised to be back for one, so if you get here about twelve we'll have time for a glass of wine and a chinwag. There's someone I'd like you to meet.'

I said nothing. I'd learned long ago that was the best course. I just hoped this one wasn't as bad as the last one, who had been six feet two to my five feet two, and it had quickly become apparent that our height wasn't the only thing we didn't have in common. Reginald was everything I most disliked in a man and could bore for

England. What on earth Denise was thinking, I had no idea, but the lack of suitable and single men in my age range had her clutching at straws, I supposed.

'I'd better go,' I said, when a response was clearly expected, 'I'm in the middle of some painting.'

'Ooh, when did you take that up? Water colour or oils?'

'Neither,' I said wryly, 'it's the ceiling in my hallway and I wasn't thinking of emulating the Sistine chapel, so it's just white emulsion.'

She laughed, 'Well, I'm impressed. Good luck with it, Jo.'

I replaced the receiver, and slumped back against the wall, feeling as if my get-up-and-go had up and left the minute I stopped working. All I wanted to do was get into bed; any previous enthusiasm for painting had evaporated the minute I realized nothing could be done the following day.

Why couldn't I just have cried off from the lunch? I could have said I was unwell, could even have told the truth and just said I wanted to get on now that I'd made a start. Denise would have understood, she was nothing if not fair.

Amenable, that was me to a 'T'. I seemed to have spent my whole life pleasing others, going with the flow, afraid of letting anyone down. I was finally beginning to see — many years too late — that with an attitude like that the one person I was really letting down was me.

I looked up at the ceiling with its patchy coat of emulsion and realized it was going to take more than a lick of paint to put right what was wrong with my life and I suddenly didn't know if I had it in me to put in the necessary effort.

★   ★   ★

Despite a shower before I'd gone to bed and a bath when I got up, there were still stubborn traces of white emulsion to be seen, not least being a residue in my hair that a thorough shampooing had failed to remove. I picked out what I could once my hair had dried and then I popped in a few of my ancient heated rollers in an effort to tidy myself up a bit.

The effort was wasted — even I could see that. I looked what I was, a plain and ordinary middle-aged woman, carrying a bit too much weight and looking a good ten years older than I actually was.

I patted my soft grey curls, suddenly aware the perm and scrubbed clean face did nothing to help the image I presented of a woman of pensionable age, and neither did the heather-coloured sweater, tweed skirt and sensible shoes. I looked like the Queen — the real one, not Helen Mirren — and she was from a whole different generation. I couldn't help wondering why it hadn't bothered me before. Too busy with the minutiae of life to realize it was passing me by, I supposed.

'You look nice,' Denise commented as soon as I put my head round the back door with a forced and very cheery, 'Hi.'

My response was a muttered, 'Hurrumph,' which was pounced on immediately.

'What's up?'

I knew I should have tried harder, because now Denise was on to my mood she wouldn't be happy until she had the whole story and had set about putting things right. It was what she was best at, as her family would testify, and talking of family, I realized that would be a good way to distract her.

'How is Bobbi, and the baby?'

'They're fine, as well you know.' Denise looked at me sternly. 'We were only talking about them on Friday. You spoke to Bobbi on the phone yourself on Thursday. Now, are you going to tell me what's wrong or do I have to wheedle it out of you? Better out than in, as we can both testify.'

I took off my coat and, putting it on the

back of a chair, stood back, put my hands out, palms up and said, 'Look at me.'

'I am,' she said, 'and you look absolutely fine. If you ignore the splodges of emulsion you look much the same as usual, though I think you've done something with your hair and it looks rather nice.'

'Oh, stop it, Denise. I look as old and dreary as I feel. I can't even bear to look in the mirror any more. I can tart up the flat a bit but what about me?'

To her credit, Denise didn't argue. 'Well, you know I've been there, haven't I? After I lost Rob, I seriously went to pot, but that's easily rectified, you know. Look at me — even I know I look much better these days, but I'm no younger than I was then, in fact I'm a bit older. It's amazing what a change of image can do for a girl.'

'But I don't have a daughter whose clothes and make-up I can try,' I pointed out, knowing that's what had started the road to recovery for Denise, 'and I don't have a man.'

We both knew that getting together with her late husband's best friend had been the final piece in the picture of her new life. No one could have been more thrilled for her, but as I so rightly pointed out, I had no daughter and I had no man in my life.

'I know you don't have a daughter, but you

have a friend who can help,' she laughed, 'and believe me when I say it, start feeling good about yourself again and the man will follow.'

'I can't try *your* clothes on.' I indicated her trim figure and hip-skimming jeans. She did look absolutely great for a woman in her late forties and for the first time ever I was very envious of her.

'I wasn't always this size,' Denise reminded me, 'and I'm not very good at getting rid of stuff. I'll see what I can find.'

'You're telling me you're not very good at getting rid of stuff.' Adam popped his dark head round the door. 'There are enough rails of clothes in that loft to keep Oxfam going for years.' He turned to me and the smile on his face told me clearly he was happy for Denise to fill the roof right up to the rafters if it made her happy. 'I keep telling her the ceiling will cave in if she puts any more up there, but will she listen? Come on in, Max,' he encouraged over his shoulder and opened the door wider to allow the other guest to come inside.

Now he was *nice*. I was impressed in spite of myself, and in spite of my reservations about Denise's all too obvious latest attempt to 'fix me up'.

Tall, well built with close cropped grey hair and a pleasant face that looked a bit 'lived in', he was everything I might have looked for in a man — at least as far as appearance went. My heart gave a little unexpected flutter. It was the first time such a thing had happened in more years than I cared to remember.

'Max, how lovely to see you.' Denise lifted her face for his kiss, and then hastened to introduce me. 'This is my very good friend, Josephine.'

'Oh, call me Jo, please,' I urged as he shook my hand with a grip that was pleasingly dry and firm.

I realized immediately he had absolutely no interest in me. His gaze swept over me, barely registering my existence, and returned immediately back to Denise. He was polite enough through lunch, quite entertaining, in fact, but any exchanges with me were kept to the barest minimum. Max couldn't have made it clearer that he just didn't want to know. It shouldn't have hurt — but it did.

I tried not to let it get to me, and had succeeded — or so I thought — but I found when I got home that I was inclined to sit and brood until the whole episode became magnified out of all proportion. Why it should matter so much that a man I had never even met before clearly had no wish to get to know me better, I had no idea.

In the end, I got the emulsion out again and completed a second coat to the ceiling in record time. My decorating skills were definitely improving because as far as I could tell I'd made a damn fine job of it. I went to bed tired out but in a much better frame of mind and by the morning I was quite over the fact the less than charming Max had found me beneath his notice.

I was already sitting at my desk opening the post when Denise struggled through the door of the office with a black bin bag full to bursting in each hand.

'Hello, what on earth are you travelling with?'

She put them down by my desk and stopped to catch her breath. 'For you,' she indicated the bags.

I raised my eyebrows. 'Even with my hearty appetite I can't manage a packed lunch that big,' I protested.

'I had a clear-out last night,' she went on as if I hadn't spoken. 'Adam is thrilled to get some of his loft space back. Have a look and send what you don't want to Help the Aged or the Heart Foundation charity. There might just be something that suits you in there.'

'They won't fit,' I said, sounding disgruntled and ungrateful even to my own ears.

'Try them.'

She even gave me a lift home and helped me up the stairs with the bags. By the weight of them, Denise must have cleared the entire loft, but I couldn't bring myself to be pleased. I vowed, as I stuffed them out of sight, that I wasn't even going to try the clothes on, choosing instead to be offended that she obviously agreed I needed help with my wardrobe — and heaven only knew what else.

Furious, I spun on my comfortably heeled shoes and, as I came face to face with myself in the wardrobe mirror, I had to admit she was right. If the old saying, 'A man is as old as he feels and a woman is as old as she looks,' held true, I would definitely be put at least ten or even fifteen years older than my actual age. It was quite clear I hadn't so much allowed myself to slide into old age as hurtle there at breakneck speed.

With my middle-aged spread, comfortable clothes and grey curls, I bore more than a passing resemblance to my own mother in her final years — and she had been well into her eighties. No wonder Max had looked as if he was wishing himself elsewhere all through lunch.

I felt my whole body sag, then I actually watched my face crumble, and finally did what I had been wanting to do ever since I'd arrived home, and burst into tears.

# 4

How I ended up discussing the whole problem with Greg Masters, of all people, I had no idea. He turned up at the door to see how the decorating was going, stepped inside in a very obvious effort to wind up Edna, and the next minute it all came tumbling out.

'You look all right to me,' he said. He didn't sound very convincing, and I didn't think 'all right' was exactly high praise, but perhaps that was due to my heightened sensitivity so I tried not to mind. 'I expect your friend was only trying to help,' he continued sensibly, 'and it wouldn't hurt to look at the clothes, would it?'

'I don't think you understand, Greg,' I told him. 'It's not just about what you see on the outside, I am this dull and rapidly ageing person on the inside, too, and though I admit I need to change, I just don't know where to start. I've spent so long looking after everyone else and now there's just me. I'm not used to having time to put myself under the microscope like this. I've suddenly found myself with a life to live and no idea what I want to do with it.'

'I think I do understand more than you think. When my wife was ill, I gave up everything to nurse her — not just my business but my life, too. She was all I could think about and all that kept me going, then when she first died it suddenly became a huge effort to get out of bed in the morning, never mind to get through each day. I had to leave the home and the life we shared and try to start over somewhere new. It has become easier since I came here and I manage to keep busy, but there's no real purpose or meaning to my life any more and the years are slipping past, almost unnoticed.'

He stopped talking suddenly and just looked at me.

'What?' I said. 'Have you had an idea?'

'You could say that,' he nodded. 'It's great to talk and, I don't know about you, but I find I welcome the opportunity, and I was just thinking that we could be painting these walls while we talk. I'd be happy to make a start if you go and put the kettle on.'

Well, we're always being told it's good to talk and I'd obviously be doing him a favour by keeping him busy, given what he'd just said about his life having no purpose or meaning. The dustsheets were still down, so I pointed out the colour I'd picked and, leaving him to make a start, I went to make the tea.

The gleam on Edna's letterbox must have been blinding, because we were hard at work all evening. I wondered why I had been so insistent on going it alone when I saw how much could be achieved over a much shorter time with two rollers on the go. Although the walls were still a bit patchy, you could see another good coat would do it and the hall looked much brighter and smarter already.

I said as much and then added belatedly, 'You should have changed your clothes,' I pointed at the numerous splashes of emulsion decorating the disreputable track suit, 'though it might wash out.'

'Oh, these clothes have seen better days,' he shrugged, and then added, a little bit hesitantly, 'I'd been thinking lately about updating my own image a bit as well, to be honest.'

'Really?' I carefully refrained from adding that it wasn't before time. After all, who was I to talk, anyway?

'I used to be quite dapper, if that's the word. My wife saw to that before she became ill, but I haven't put on a suit in years and I doubt those I have would even fit any more.'

I forced myself to laugh, and said, 'We're a right pair, aren't we?' Greg managed a kind of lop-sided grin, but I thought he looked sad. 'We'd better start packing up before Edna rubs a hole in the door.'

He had already picked up a roller, and I took it from his hand. Slowly and deliberately, I dipped it into the paint tray and then rolled a wide strip of emulsion down the front of my sweater and skirt, clothes I had managed to keep relatively free of splashes until that moment.

'What on earth are you doing?' The expression on Greg's face was classic.

'I don't think it will wash out, do you?' I said in a troubled tone, before reaching to paint a similar stripe on the front of his tatty tracksuit. 'Or that?'

Stunned for just a few seconds, the next minute the other roller was in his hand, replenished with paint and rolled the length of my back. I flicked my roller in his direction and he flicked his in mine. Before long we were covered in emulsion and laughing helplessly. I hadn't laughed that much since before the day I married Jack Farrell and it felt strange but so good.

Catching my breath, I said, 'I've never done anything so ridiculous in my life but I wasn't thinking about what would happen next. I don't think you can wear those clothes out of here, Greg. You'll get paint everywhere.'

'What?' Greg tried and failed to look affronted. 'Mrs Farrell, are you intending to send me out of here naked? Poor Edna might never recover.'

'It's late,' I pointed out helpfully and hopefully, 'she'll probably be in bed.'

'Not while she knows I'm still in here.' He was trying not to smile, but we both knew we were in trouble.

'I'll get a black bin bag for the ruined clothes and see what I can find in the back of the wardrobe.' I slipped off my shoes and walked carefully into the kitchen, returning with a roll of bags in one hand, instructing sternly, 'Turn your back and no peeking,' before removing everything except the no-nonsense underwear that wouldn't have inflamed anything except an already raging bonfire.

In the bedroom, I pulled on the comfy towelling robe that had seen better days and a pair of fluffy slippers. A search in the depths of the wardrobe produced a similar man's robe in navy blue and a pair of monster slippers that had once belonged to Petie.

I stood in the doorway, holding them out and said with a shrug, 'Best I could do, I'm afraid,' and rolling the dustsheets back a little, I suggested, 'You can stand on this bit, once you've changed, and then we can roll a clear path for you to get to the door. I'll go and put the kettle on for cocoa.'

I closed the door behind me firmly, and

found myself humming as I filled two mugs and put chocolate digestives on a plate.

'I've put all of our clothes into a bag and tied the top.' Greg stood hesitating in the doorway. 'I don't think they're fit for much now.'

'Probably not a good idea to put them out for charity then?' I held out a steaming mug and he ventured further into the room, taking the cup in one hand and a digestive in the other. 'Suits you, sir.' I indicated the clothes he wore, still shabby, and probably smelling faintly of mothballs, but the robe still made a pleasant change from the tracksuit.

'I haven't been in a paint fight since school,' Greg said. 'I don't know what came over me.'

'Actually,' I reminded him, 'it was me who started it, and I haven't laughed like that since school. It actually felt pretty good.'

He smiled then, quite shyly, and agreed, 'I thought so, too.'

I returned the smile and it felt as if something had changed between us, that we had — as unlikely as I would once have thought it — become friends.

I sat down and indicated the other chair. 'I suppose that's what they mean by 'getting old being compulsory, but growing up being optional'. I'm very fed up with acting my age,

Greg, because I seem to have been getting old for a hell of a long time and grown-up forever.'

Greg prepared to leave soon after, with my front door key in his pocket and his promise that he would have another coat on the wall before I got home from work ringing in my ear. I didn't hesitate to accept the offer of help, having already discovered that being independent was far from all it was cracked up to be.

I went first to take a quick look outside on the landing and was able to report no sign of Edna. However, I can only assume she was sitting on a chair just inside her door with the letterbox propped open, because the minute Greg stepped outside in the towelled robe it snapped shut with a bang. There was a muffled shriek, which might have indicated a pinched finger or two if Edna had got what she so richly deserved.

There was no doubt she was going to have a field day. Seeing us standing there wearing dressing gowns, she must have thought all her Christmases had come at once. We stared at each other in horror and then the humour of the situation asserted itself and once we started laughing there was just no stopping. I could hear Greg chuckling all the way down the stairs and he was still laughing when he closed his front door. For the first time in a very long time I went to bed smiling myself — though I wasn't at all sure why when my reputation was obviously going to be in shreds.

★  ★  ★

When I was telling Denise about it the next day, she laughed so hard she almost choked on the bourbon biscuit she'd just bitten into. I tried not to mind that she found it all so funny, but I did, even though I had thought it amusing myself only the evening before.

'I'm a respectable woman,' I said indignantly, 'with not one black mark against my name. I've never even had a speeding ticket.'

'That could be because you don't drive,' Denise pointed out with annoying accuracy, 'but I'm beginning to think there's something of a dark horse about you. If I'm finding it difficult to believe there's an innocent explanation for a strange man leaving your flat late at night in his dressing gown, you can bet your sweet life that Elsie — '

'Edna,' I corrected feebly.

'I stand corrected,' she accepted, continuing, 'Edna will find it impossible.'

'But there *is* an innocent explanation,' I protested.

'I know there is and I fully accept your version of events because I know you so well, but I think Edna is going to take a *lot* more convincing. You've gained a reputation overnight, my lady, and if I were you I'd make the most of it. You've been squeaky clean for far too long.'

Denise was right, I acknowledged, as I walked home at the end of the working day with a spring in my step that hadn't been there for longer than I cared to remember. For the first time in years I felt as if I was an interesting person — even if it was only to someone like Edna — and even if it was all built on a complete lie.

Two of my neighbours, who had previously scarcely shared the time of day with me, suddenly seemed inclined to engage me in conversation, but for once I was in a hurry to get home. Not only was I keen to see what Greg had accomplished, I was also mindful of the fish and chips I'd just purchased and eager they should be enjoyed while they were still piping hot.

However, walking in the door of my flat wasn't like coming home — not to my home. The hallway was *beautiful* and I stood with my mouth open, the fish and chips were forgotten.

I couldn't think how Greg had done it in

the time. The walls were a beautiful rich and even cream, but that wasn't all, the doors and skirting board had all been freshly painted white and the overall effect was light, bright and stunning.

The man himself appeared, wearing the same towelling robe, and asked with a smile, 'Is there any chance that's fish and chips I can smell because I'm absolutely starving?' Before I could find my voice he went on, 'I hope you don't mind that I used your shower, and the bath robe and slippers again, too?'

'Oh, God, no, of course not, I can't believe how much you've done today. It looks fantastic, Greg, I can't thank you enough. Fish and chips seems a very poor way of showing my gratitude.'

'According to Edna, I've already been amply rewarded with far more than cod and chips.'

'Greg!' I was shocked. 'Please don't tell me she's actually been telling people we're having an affair?'

He looked rueful. 'I'm afraid we can count on it. She's been scuttling round the flats at such a speed you could see sparks flying from her heels. I'm so sorry, Jo.'

I found myself staring at him. 'Why are you apologizing, Greg? You have nothing to be sorry about. Your behaviour has never been less than impeccable. It's Edna who should be ashamed, jumping to conclusions like that, but do you know what?'

Greg shook his head, pulling a no idea face.

'Denise was right — she's my boss and friend — ' I added by way of an explanation, 'when she said I'd been squeaky clean for far too long. No one has found anything interesting to say about me since I was caught having a crafty fag — and it took me years to give up incidentally — behind the bike sheds in secondary school. I should be thanking you for finally giving me a reputation, but I do apologize that lending a neighbourly hand has made you the butt of Edna's spiteful gossip.'

'Shall we eat those fish and chips while they're still reasonably hot?'

Greg reached out to take the securely wrapped package and made his way to the kitchen. I trailed after him, almost, I thought, as if he was the host and I was the guest. He compounded that impression by using my kitchen as if it was his own while I hung around like a spare part and in no time we were seated at the table and munching away in companionable silence.

'I only ever have salt on chips, never with anything else,' I said around a mouthful of crisply battered cod, wondering even as I said it why I thought he would find that fact even remotely interesting.

'Same here with vinegar,' Greg proved the point by adding even more to the pile of chips on his plate, and I realized that friends did talk about inconsequential things. Denise and I did it all the time. How else would you discover each other's likes and dislikes?

I finally sat back with a huge satisfied sigh and finally felt able to ask, 'So what do we do about Edna, then?'

'Why would we bother to do anything? We've done nothing wrong, and if we start protesting it might look as if we have something to hide.'

'Mmm. A couple of the neighbours tried to start a conversation with me outside, the first time I've been offered more than a brief greeting by anyone other than Edna in all the years I've lived here.'

'How long have you lived here, if you don't mind me asking.'

'I came here as a newly wed when I married Jack, more years ago than I care to remember, then when I was left on my own with Peter my mother moved in to help out. She wasn't the easiest person to get along with and neither was Jack.'

Greg took a sip of his tea and looked at me over the brim of the mug.

I suddenly felt compelled to be honest, 'It was never going to be the best marriage. Jack was an alcoholic — though I didn't realize it at the time. My relationship with my mother always left a lot to be desired but she thought the world of Peter and that was all that mattered.'

'They're both gone now, are they?'

'Oh, yes, a good few years ago. I don't miss either of them, but by then I had Petie's teenage years to contend with.'

'He's your son,' Greg hazarded a guess, adding, 'I think I've seen him coming and going. Good-looking lad. A bit of a handful, was he?'

I nodded, loyalty preventing me from saying more.

'That's children for you, I suppose. Families often bring problems but I envy you your son. Monica and I would have liked children but it just never happened for us.'

'Petie kept me sane through the bad times. He was a lovely little boy and only went off the rails after his Dad and then his Gran . . . you know. He's turned his life around now, though, and I couldn't be more proud of him.' I found myself smiling at the thought of him, and then added, 'I would like to make

56

him proud of me, too.'

Greg gave me a straight look. 'I'm sure he is already. Just having three generations living in the same flat must have been murder at times. Obviously, I don't know all that much about you and your circumstances, but there's no doubt in my mind that you must have kept the family going through what would have been some difficult times.'

'That's what women do, isn't it? Like most women my age, I feel a bit redundant now that nobody depends on me. That's why I would like to do something that will make me proud of myself, something that reminds me I do still have a life.'

'You have your list,' Greg reminded me, 'and, according to Edna you're already having an affair — and that wasn't even on it. If my memory serves me right you've also made a start on number eight, too.'

'Number eight?' I repeated faintly, trying and failing to recall anything at all from that original list.

'Move or decorate?'

'Oh, yes.' I was inordinately pleased to think I had actually made a start, even if I had all but forgotten what had originally prodded me into action in the first place. In fairness I felt I should add, 'but you actually did most of the decorating and I would like to pay you for your time.'

'You will *not*,' Greg's tone was emphatic. 'You've done me a massive favour allowing me to get involved, got me out of the huge rut I had dug myself into in the years following Monica's death *and* given me a racy reputation. I should actually be paying *you*.'

'You don't get out of it that easily,' I gave him a frowning look, just to show I meant business. 'There must be something I can do for you.'

'We-ell.' The word was pulled out reluctantly and hung there between us.

I quailed and suddenly baulked at the thought of what he might be about to ask of me. Whatever it was, I had brought this onto myself, and for a horrified moment it went through my mind that Greg might be going to ask me to make our pretend affair into a real one — and I knew that was the one thing I couldn't do.

# 5

The moment lengthened until the silence was almost unbearable, and all the while I could feel a refusal edging its way to the tip of my tongue.

Finally, Greg spoke and he pleaded, 'Please don't laugh at me,' and I felt physically sick at the way I was going to have to rebuff him and signal the end of a friendship that had come to mean an awful lot to me in a ridiculously short time.

'I won't laugh,' I was able to promise with conviction and without hesitation, and then found myself doing just that when he said with a sheepish grin, 'Help me to make a list like yours.'

I watched his face fall and immediately regretted what I recognized as misplaced humour, because to Greg this was obviously no laughing matter.

'I'm sorry, I'm sorry.' I caught at his hand and held it tight. 'Of course I will help you to write your list. I'm flattered that you should ask me and I promise I will take the responsibility very seriously.'

'You're still laughing at me,' he accused,

but there was a definite twinkle in his eye and a twitch to his lips.

'I promise you I am not. We're friends, aren't we? And friends can ask each other anything without fear of ridicule. You barely knew me when you helped with my list and that, without a doubt, was the start of our friendship. To be honest, it was the first time I saw you as anything other than a grumpy old bugger.'

'A grumpy old — ' Greg looked less than impressed.

'I didn't know you then. Now I realize you were just unhappy and still grieving and that's taught me not to be so judgemental. Go on then,' I offered.

He lifted a shoulder, his expression blank.

'You can tell me your impression of me and I promise I won't be offended. I can't be any fairer than that,' I finished, bracing myself for his honest verdict.

'I thought you worked hard, long hours sometimes, and that you often looked tired. If I'm honest I also wondered what you found to do with your spare time — seeing that I found it so hard to fill mine — because you seemed to spend an awful lot of time alone in your flat when you weren't working. Not that I was watching you,' he hastened to add, 'but you do tend to notice the comings and goings of neighbours when you have too much time on your hands. You only have to look at Edna.'

'Mmm,' I mused, 'I suppose we should have more compassion. After all, while she's busily shredding our reputations, she's not only enjoying herself, but leaving someone else alone.'

We both laughed, and Greg said, 'I suppose I should feel flattered she thinks I still have it in me to attract a lady.'

'Oh, me, too,' I agreed, 'attract a man, I mean.'

'Have you got a piece of paper handy?'

'What?' I began, and then smiled, 'Oh, for the list. Crumbs, you're eager,' and went to the kitchen drawer for the pad I always kept there.

'Number one,' he said firmly and without any hesitation, 'fall in love again.'

My mouth fell open. 'Well, you don't mess about, do you, mister?'

'I've been on my own now for three years, Jo, and I hate it. I have a lot of love to give to the right person and I'm positive it's what Monica would want for me.'

I was sure he was right, but how could you tell a friend that the way he looked he was never going to attract anyone, let alone the special someone he was obviously hoping for.

'Oh, I'm sure you're right,' I agreed, and mindful of his feelings, continued, 'but I think you're rushing ahead a bit. You haven't even been on a date yet, and where are you going to meet this 'right person', Greg?'

'I was hoping you would tell me that.'

'Me? But I've been on my own far longer that you have and, despite Denise's best efforts to fix me up, here I still am.'

Greg gave me a straight look that went on and on. It was clear he wanted to say something, but wasn't quite sure whether he should.

'What?' I said, and then again more forcefully, 'What?'

'I don't quite know how to say this and I'm a bit worried about how you will take it, but we are friends now — '

'Oh, for God's sake,' I was becoming quite nettled, wondering what on earth he was going to say, 'just spit it out, why don't you?'

'We-ell, you did say you wanted to update your image — number four on your list — and to be truthful, it's not before time. You don't exactly make the best of yourself, do you?' he said bluntly and then flinched as I yelled, 'What?'

'Well, look at yourself,' he encouraged, 'go on, really take a long hard look,' and getting to his feet he went into the hall and came back with the full-length mirror that had been screwed to the wall until it was taken down for the wall to be painted.

Damn him, he stood there holding the bloody mirror right in front of me, urging me to 'stand up, go on, stand up and look'.

I had little choice in the matter, and he knew it, because if I refused to look I was still playing right into his hands.

'There's nothing wrong with what I'm wearing. It's perfectly respectable,' I said defensively, eyeing the navy jumper and matching pleated skirt.

'Yes,' Greg allowed, 'but it's very middle-aged and staid, more suited to someone at least ten years older.'

'You don't know how old I am,' I pointed out, scowling at my sensible shoes.

'Too old for mini skirts, but too young for pleats and pinafore dresses is my guess,' he said with a wry touch of humour, 'and then there's the hair.'

Before I could stop myself a hand crept up to touch the grey curls, 'I am *not* dying my hair.'

'Fair enough, but a *perm*, Jo? Honestly.'

I think it was the smirk that did it, but I lost it then, totally lost it. '*When* you've quite finished,' I fumed, barely preventing myself from putting a well-aimed foot through the mirror he was still holding, 'picking *my* appearance to bits, perhaps I can have my say about *yours*.'

'Mine?' Greg looked surprised.

'Yes, bloody yours. You have the gall, the barefaced cheek to have a go at me, looking the way you do.'

'What's wrong . . . ?'

' . . . with you? What's bloody right would be nearer the mark. Give me the damn mirror, go on give it to me and then take a long hard look at yourself. In your mind's eye replace the towelling robe and slippers with those bloody horrible tracksuits you live in, and the scruffy old trainers. And the hair — well — how you have the nerve to criticize mine I will never know.'

Almost panting, we stood and glared at each other, all the good feeling between us evaporating almost tangibly until there was nothing good left at all and I was too furious even to care.

'Thank you for the fish and chips and for your honesty — even if I do consider it a little harsh,' Greg said stiffly.

'Thank you for the painting effort *and* for the criticism that you clearly see as constructive but I can't help feeling is destructive.'

I was equally formal in my response and

willing Greg to leave before I gave him the satisfaction of seeing me crumble as the initial rush of anger drained away. A confidence that had always been fragile, thanks to the years of being put down by a husband determined to keep me in my allotted place at the bottom of the pecking order within the family, had been splintered thanks to his thoughtless words and I didn't think I could ever forgive him for that. The fact I'd managed to get my own back in a small way didn't help one little bit.

He left without another word. I was glad to see him go and rued the day I had let my guard slip long enough to allow him into my life. With friends like that who on earth needed enemies? A tear slipped down my cheek and I scrubbed it away angrily and went to put the kettle on.

After two cups of tea I had calmed down a bit and turned my energies to clearing away the dustsheets and decorating paraphernalia in the hall and then stood back to admire the finished picture. I felt a twinge of regret that I hadn't been more effusive in my appreciation of Greg's efforts, but pushed the thought away and considered instead my options regarding the shabby carpet that was presently spoiling the whole effect of the smooth cream walls and gleaming paintwork.

A new carpet would have been my preferred choice, or even laminate flooring, but the thought of the cost, and the upheaval of tearing up the old floor covering and disposing of it, put me off before I even started. Shampooing the carpet wasn't ideal as it had seen better days and certainly wasn't going to last forever, but it would have to do. Perhaps a couple of strategically placed rugs would hide the worst of the worn patches and, best of all as far as I was concerned, I could manage a bit of carpet sprucing all by myself.

★　★　★

Greg stayed right out of my way. Whether by accident, or design on his part — the latter probably the more likely — I didn't set eyes on him for several weeks and in that time the hall was completed to my satisfaction. I then managed to clear the boxroom of its clutter before painting the ceiling, walls and paintwork and, pleased with the result, was preparing to move into the second bedroom so that I could start work on mine.

'It's a big job to tackle alone, Jo. Why not let me come and lend a hand and borrow Adam to move the furniture?'

Denise was obviously concerned but I chose to see it as criticism and almost snapped her head off. I apologized almost immediately. In truth, I couldn't deny it was all getting too much for me, though that was something I would only admit to myself and I had no intention of stopping now the flat was starting to look so good.

The fact was, I'd gone from doing precious little with my time outside of the office to working all the hours God sent, falling into bed exhausted every night. I couldn't remember the last time I'd eaten a decent meal, but thought it was probably the fish and chips, and I wished again that particular evening hadn't ended so acrimoniously. Reminding myself that Greg had started it didn't bring the usual swift rush of anger and I was forced to acknowledge that I missed the bloody man — though I was damned if I would admit it to anyone but myself.

★　★　★

After my success with the boxroom, I'd been gradually clearing the drawers and wardrobe space in the second bedroom to make space for my own and, after checking with Petie, anything of his went to the nearest charity shop, along with several items I'd found belonging to my mother and even one or two things of Jack's.

I discovered it was true what they said about decluttering your life in those television programmes about the subject, it *was* liberating to let go of the past and bury the bad memories deep in the bags destined to be shared among various good causes as I dropped them off one at a time on my way to work each morning.

Now the room was clear, I was tempted to start in there, but my own room was definitely the better of the two and I was itching to give it a real make-over, continuing the light and bright theme started in the hallway. I might even get myself a little TV set — I'd seen second hand ones advertised for as little as ten pounds — so that I could snuggle up in bed to watch a late night film now and again. I shook my head, finally accepting my life and home were my own to do with as I decided, with no one to please but myself.

In my own bedroom I was faced with the bags Denise had given me weeks before, and I tutted as I pulled them out into the room from the corner where I had dumped them. While I was decluttering I would sort out my own clothes and I might just as well look through these while I was at it, though I'd be surprised if there was anything in there that could possibly be of use to me.

Five minutes later I was staring at myself in the speckled mirror of the ancient wardrobe, my mouth a round 'O' of surprise, my head shaking as I repeated over and over again, 'I don't believe it, I don't believe it,' fully aware I was sounding just like the character Victor Meldrew from the television series *One Foot In The Grave*.

I was hardly skinny, but had definitely lost a bit of weight. It was a fact I could only put down to the work I was putting in around the flat, which had also left me with less time for comfort eating. The plain black trouser suit and white blouse took pounds off me, not to mention years. I looked quite shapely and much closer to my real age, especially when I brushed my hair a bit flatter and tucked it behind my ears.

Much as I hated to admit it, Greg had been right, and it was only fair that I told him so. I felt far too good to keep the transformation to myself and I was halfway down the stairs before I could change my mind and perhaps think twice about it. I already had my hand raised to knock on Greg's door when it opened as if by magic.

'Jo,' he said his face lighting up, 'I was just on my way up to you.'

'You were?'

'You look . . . ' Greg hesitated, '*different*.'

'So,' I murmured, looking him up and down, 'do you.'

A slight noise made us look up, and it immediately became clear to us both that we needed to make a move or Edna would be in grave danger of falling over the stair rail in her efforts to listen in on our conversation.

'Will you come in?' Greg sounded almost nervous.

'I think I'd better,' I whispered, with a wry smile, adding, 'before Edna breaks her neck. Thanks, Greg,' I said loudly, 'let's go and put the kettle on, shall we?'

With the door safely shut behind us, we stopped, stared at each other and took stock. I was well aware of the change in my own appearance, achieved with little more than a set of second-hand clothes and a hairbrush, but took the opportunity to take a good long look at Greg.

Not much change with his hairstyle, which was still too long and straggly for my taste, but his clothes, though still on the casual side, were a vast improvement on the tatty track-suit. Navy slacks and light-blue sweater, with the collar of a navy shirt setting off the V neck, and polished black slip-ons replacing the battered trainers had made a world of difference to his appearance. There was obviously some truth in the saying that *clothes maketh man* — and woman.

'Wow,' I said, and realized Greg had said the same thing at the same time. We both laughed and it felt as if the ice between us was finally melting, as was proved by his next words.

'I'm sorry, Jo. I shouldn't have taken umbrage at what were, after all, just honest comments and, if I was a bit brutal about your appearance, I apologize for that, too. It wasn't my intention to upset you.'

'I realize that and also that I have difficulty accepting criticism, but there are reasons and they go back such a long way that it's difficult to change.'

'I guess we've both been a bit battered by life,' Greg said ruefully.

I guess you're right, but the past is past and it's time for a new start — for both of us. Now,' I pushed him along in front of me towards the sitting room and, when we got there, I continued, 'about that list. I think we were about to decide on number two, weren't we?'

It was easier said than done. The only thing he did with any conviction was to fetch a pen and piece of paper. I'd thought I was indecisive, but as I watched Greg struggle I realized I didn't know the true meaning of the word. Using my list as a template clearly wasn't going to work as a trigger, either, since updating our image was probably the only thing on it that could be applied to both of us.

'I don't *have* to have ten things on the list, do I?' Greg looked so horrified at the idea that I burst out laughing, and immediately apologized.

'It was the look on your face,' I explained, 'but of course you don't have to have ten. This is your list. You can have as many or as few as you want. Look, I'll put the heading.'

GREG'S LIST

I wrote the title boldly at the top of the sheet in the centre and then underneath I wrote the only item we had to start us off.

1. Fall in love (At least I thought he was in with a reasonable chance now he'd made an effort with his appearance though I refrained from saying so).

'OK,' I looked at him with the pen poised, 'it's up to you.'

He suddenly smiled and, with relief clear in his tone, he said happily, 'Well, my number two is your number four — 'update image'. It doesn't matter that

I've already started, does it?'

Feeling inordinately pleased for him, I put it on the list and told him, 'I would say that's a plus, wouldn't you?' I began to tick the things from my list off on my fingers in an effort to move things along. 'Learning to drive is a no, because you already do. Learning to sew?' I looked at him quizzically.

Greg pulled a face. 'I can sew a button on and even put a stitch in a hem when required, but I don't see myself wanting to run up a ball gown any time soon, to be honest.'

'OK,' I nodded, continuing ruthlessly, 'decorate cakes,' I ticked that off my finger quickly and confirmed, 'update image we already have.'

'Hold on, go back.'

'To . . . ?'

'Decorate cakes — I wouldn't dismiss that one out of hand. I already make them, don't I?'

'Good thinking, I'll put that as your number three, then, shall I?'

'Yes, go on.' He looked quite taken with the idea.

'Learn to do something artistic?'

'Isn't decorating cakes artistic?'

'I was thinking more of painting or writing?' I pointed out.

Greg screwed up his nose. 'Not really me,' he said.

'Fine, and holidaying abroad you've already done, so we can forget that one,' I dismissed, and went on to query, 'Diet?'

'Go back to holidaying abroad.'

'You don't want to diet?'

'I'm not saying that. I'll think about that one in a minute. I have holidayed abroad, but there are places I haven't been that I might like to try. What about making number four, holidaying somewhere new? It doesn't even have to be abroad.'

'Ah, you see, you're getting the hang of this now, aren't you?' I found myself beaming at Greg. 'Now, what about diet, or do you think you're perfect as you are?' I carefully refrained from looking at a quite pronounced paunch, reminding myself that it was up to him.

'Can we call it healthy eating? I know I would benefit from losing a few pounds, but I hate the word diet. It conjures up lettuce, carrots and — ugh — celery. Anyway, I can see you've lost weight. Tell me how that happened? Did you start number seven while we weren't speaking?'

'No, but I did get on with some decorating, which left me with no time to sit around and comfort eat. Also my decluttering efforts have meant lugging bin bags of discarded items to various charity shops. I guess it's been a combination of eating less and exercising more. I didn't even notice the weight coming off until I tried this suit on.'

'Let's call it healthy living, then, shall we?' Greg suggested. 'I don't fancy joining a gym but I don't object to walking more. As it is, I use the car to go ridiculously short distances. Walking will do me good and save money at the same time.'

I added healthy living to the list and moved swiftly on, feeling encouraged with the way things were going. 'Move house or decorate?' I looked around the room we were sitting in, but I didn't need to. 'I don't know if you were thinking of moving house, but this place certainly doesn't need decorating.'

'Can we put helping you with yours on my list?'

'But I'm trying to be independent,' I pointed out.

He came straight back with, 'That's not on your list, is it? And if you try to do everything yourself you'll never tick anything else off the list. Go on, Jo, it's helped *you* lose weight, so it would probably do the same for *me*.'

'Well, if you put it like that.' I liked the way he made it look as if I was doing him a favour. 'Shall we put number six as helping the neighbours, then?'

'As long as I get to choose which neighbours I help,' he frowned and flicked his gaze toward the ceiling.

'It's your list,' I reminded him. 'Now, do you fancy getting your ears pierced?' Greg shook his head emphatically, and I counted off the final one from my list. 'Visit a clairvoyant?'

'Load of mumbo-jumbo,' he dismissed.

'How do you know if you've never visited one?' I countered, 'or have you?'

'No, I haven't.'

'Well, then.' I hadn't ever visited a clairvoyant either, but I wasn't about to dismiss them or their talents out of hand and I could confess to being curious. However, I changed the subject, sensing a subject we might disagree upon. 'If you've finished with this list, is there any chance of getting a cup of tea around here? I'm parched.'

'I'll put the kettle on, while you write the list out properly,' he indicated the paper with its mainly indecipherable scribble and scratched out words and numbers. Reminding me, 'Yours doesn't look like that.'

Obediently, I began again as he went off to the kitchen.

## GREG'S LIST

1. Fall in love
2. Update image
3. Learn to decorate cakes
4. Holiday somewhere new
5. Healthy living
6. Help the neighbour(s)

I looked up to find that Greg had come back into the room and was standing looking at me. He looked at if he wanted to say something, but didn't quite know how it would be received.

'What?' I asked, and then more sharply when he still didn't speak, 'What? And where's the tea I was promised?'

'Erm,' he began and then stopped again, before saying in a rush, 'I was wondering whether you might not prefer a real drink.'

'All right.' I thought that sounded reasonable. 'What have you got?'

'Erm, I actually meant — would you fancy going out for one? With me?'

# 6

I was speechless. Greg had only asked me to
go for a drink. People got asked to go out for
a drink all the time — but not me. The last
man to invite me out for a drink had been
Jack Farrell, so long ago that I didn't care to
remember, and look where accepting that
invitation had got me. I had no intention of
getting involved with my downstairs neighbour. He wasn't my type, though exactly what
my type was I actually had no idea and,
anyway, I wasn't the one looking for love.

Greg had hesitated before he made his
request and now it was my turn to hesitate as
I searched for a polite way to tell him to just
go and put the bloody kettle on and forget
anything else.

To my amazement he suddenly burst out
laughing, and said, 'You should see your face,
Jo. It's a drink, nothing more, and nothing
less. We're friends, aren't we? I just thought it
would be nice, since we've both made an
effort with our appearance. There's no way
I'd go out on my own and you probably feel
exactly the same. Going together will give us
both a bit of confidence and it would be a

step towards the kind of social life most normal people enjoy.'

I felt all the tension go out of me with a whoosh and smiled. I couldn't quite bring myself to laugh, though I should have — at my own stupidity. I also felt a bit embarrassed that Greg had so easily read what was in my mind.

'You're right, of course. Now I feel silly.'

'Don't. With Edna spreading the news of our 'affair' I wouldn't blame you if you flatly refused to be seen with me in public.'

'That would be playing right into her hands, though, wouldn't it? Look as if we're hiding away. This way we'll be showing we have nothing to hide.'

'Exactly,' Greg gave a satisfied nod. 'We don't need coats, do we? It's a mild evening.'

'Oh, I don't have any money with me,' I patted my empty pockets — well, technically, they were Denise's pockets — in a helpless kind of way. 'I'll have to pop upstairs for my purse.'

'Come on,' he crooked an arm for me to slide my hand through, 'if I can't treat my friend to a drink it's a pretty poor state of affairs — if you'll excuse the pun. You can return the favour another time.'

We clattered down the stairs, mindful of Edna's yellow duster fluttering back and forth along the banister rail above us. Realizing she was going to have an absolute field day with us going out on what she would be convinced was a date, I think we both agreed, without the need for words, that she couldn't be allowed to make us feel guilty for the friendship we'd found so unexpectedly.

With a nod to our new way of life and Greg's 'healthy living' objective, we walked to the nearest pub instead of going further afield by car. I had been inside that particular hostelry more than once before. Denise and I had lunched at most of the locals during the long working life we shared, and I'd even met Petie for a drink a time or two, but walking through the door during the evening in the company of a man was a whole new experience, I found, and one I really enjoyed.

For once I felt as if I fitted in, and wasn't the one wearing the exclamation mark above her head proclaiming, 'Poor woman all on her own,' and not, 'Single and independent,' which would have been more apt and infinitely more preferable.

'What can I get for you?' Greg looked totally comfortable leaning on the bar, with a ten-pound note in his hand.

'Oh, I don't know,' I shrugged, 'orange juice or something.'

'You don't want the 'real drink',' he made

quote marks with his fingers, 'that we came out for?'

'Does that bother you?'

He held up both hands, the note still held in one, 'Not if orange juice is *really* your preferred choice,' he said.

I glanced over my shoulder to see who was listening, but no one was showing the least interest in our conversation, so I gave in and admitted, 'To be honest I don't know what a 'real drink' is. Does wine count, because I do have the occasional glass of white?'

'Great. Pinot Grigio suit you, or perhaps Chardonnay?'

I was relieved to hear something I recognized. 'Yes, that, the first one, will be lovely, thank you. Oh, look, there's a table. Shall I nab it and leave you to bring the drinks over?'

I moved quickly, but not quickly enough and another, slightly younger woman, reached it at the same time as I did. I turned away with a smile to show there were no hard feelings.

'Do you want to share? There are four chairs, so you and your husband could join me and mine.'

By the time I'd turned back, the lady was pulling out a chair for me and she patted the seat invitingly.

'Oh, are you sure?' I didn't quite know how

to explain that Greg wasn't my husband, so I didn't. It wasn't really important to confide in a complete stranger and our exact relationship could be clarified later if necessary as far as I was concerned.

'Haven't see you in here before, have I?' she was nosy but in a friendly kind of way. 'Keith and I come in all the time. It gets us away from the telly.'

I sat down and, making a determined effort to be sociable, told her, 'I usually only come in on a lunchtime with my friend.'

'Oh, he's not your husband, then?'

Well, I thought, pleased, *that* was cleared up without any effort on my part. Aloud I said, 'No, Greg isn't my husband, or even my boyfriend.'

'I'm surprised,' she said, 'because I thought you looked really nice together — like a couple should.'

Which meant what, I wondered, not sure whether to be pleased or offended. I realized Greg had improved on the way he dressed, but that hair . . .

The two men had obviously been chatting at the bar and now they walked over together carrying the drinks, taking the seats on the opposite side of the table.

'I'm Keith, my wife is Pauline, and this is Greg,' Keith started the introductions, and I

82

filled in the gap with, 'I'm Jo.'

It was surprisingly pleasant just to sit and chat about this and that, everything and nothing at all and I couldn't remember enjoying an evening as much for a very long time. I really felt as if I belonged and could actually see why Greg was so keen to be part of a couple again. It hadn't bothered me much before because I'd never known what it was like to be half of a couple such as Greg and Monica must have been, and Keith and Pauline were, but just a couple of hours had shown me the benefits.

I even plucked up the courage to ask Pauline where she had her hair done. She laughed, patting her trendy, two-coloured short and spiky style self-consciously, but she looked pleased to be asked, and said, 'Oh, do you like it. Keith would prefer my hair longer, but I find it really easy to manage.'

'I love it,' I said honestly, 'and I'm looking for a change of image — something a bit more up-to-date. Do you think something similar would suit me? Though without the colours, as I don't think I could carry that off as well as you.' I added the latter tactfully, not wishing to offend, but realizing without a doubt that the blonde style with darker hair at the back was definitely not for me.

'Only one way to find out,' Pauline said.

'The one good thing about hair is that if you make a mistake it grows back in no time. Yours is a great colour, too, really silvery and not salt and pepper grey.'

'So you wouldn't recommend a colour on it, then?'

She eyed me speculatively, and then shook her head. 'I don't think so. I think a change of style will be enough to give you a real lift and, to be honest,' she patted her own blonde hair again, 'coloured hair can be more trouble than it's worth, especially when it's two-tone like this. I'm always having mine retouched. Look, I'll give you the name of my hairdresser.

\* \* \*

'I really enjoyed that,' I told Greg as we made our way back home. I was quite comfortable taking his arm this time, probably relaxed by the three glasses of wine I'd imbibed. 'What a nice friendly couple. Pauline even gave me the number for her hairdresser.'

The look Greg gave me was quizzical. 'Going the whole hog are you?' he asked, adding hastily, 'Not that it's any of my business.'

I laughed, 'You don't think her choice of colours will suit me?' Without giving him the chance to reply, I continued, 'Nor do I, as it

84

happens, but I do fancy something short and a bit trendy. As Pauline said, at least with hair if you don't like it, it will soon grow back.'

'I can't wait to see it.' Greg was smiling and, smiling back, I felt able to add, 'You don't fancy a change of style then? Something like Keith's, perhaps?'

'Are you trying to say I could do with a haircut?' Greg was still smiling, so he obviously hadn't taken offence, and I was relieved. I did notice that he smoothed his hair selfconsciously, though.

'It's very fashionable at the moment for men to sport cropped hair,' I pointed out, gaining courage.

'We called it a crew cut in my day,' he said wryly, 'and I don't fancy that look at all for myself. However,' he went on, before I could speak, 'I do think you're probably right. I could do with a decent haircut.'

We parted with a cheery 'Goodnight' on Greg's landing, after I assured him very seriously that there was really no need to walk me home. As I closed my front door behind me, I called, 'Goodnight, Miss Gutheridge,' and went inside laughing when she obviously forgot I wasn't supposed to realize she was watching out for me, and replied, 'Goodnight', through the letterbox without thinking.

I said not a word to Denise the following day about the changes I was about to make, but carried on wearing my own clothes — even though it irked me — until the hairdresser Pauline had recommended could fit me in. Luckily, I didn't have long to wait and she came around one evening only a week later.

I took to Tina immediately, liking the way she listened carefully to my own ideas and then made a few thoughtful suggestions of her own.

'I think you can get away with a very short, almost urchin-type cut,' she nodded, 'which will get rid of most of the perm. I think that alone will take years off you — not that you look old,' she added hastily, 'but perms are a bit passé now, unless you're a member of the blue-rinse brigade.'

Shampooed and caped with Tina hovering over me with the scissors in her hand, I had a moment of grave doubt. 'What if I don't like it?' I murmured fearfully.

She laughed. 'I wish I had a pound for every time a customer said that to me. I'd be very rich. You'll love it, and even if you don't, it . . . '

' . . . will soon grow back,' I finished for her.

'Exactly, but it's up to you.'

I closed my eyes and crossed my fingers

under the cape. 'Go ahead,' I told her, hearing a firmness in my tone that I was far from feeling.

Grey curls fell on and around me and, eventually, the trepidation went away and excitement took over. I'd wanted to change and, by golly, this was going to be one of the biggest for me. I wasn't going to be sorry to see the back of those heated rollers, either.

'You've gone very quiet,' Tina said. 'Do you want to have a look now?'

'Is it finished?' I shook my head. 'It feels very light.'

She removed the cape and began to sweep up the hair, despite my protestations that she really shouldn't bother, leaving me to make my way to the hall mirror.

'Oh,' I gasped, and took a step back. For a long moment I was too shocked to speak, and I could see Tina peering anxiously round the kitchen door behind me. 'It's — ' I began.

'It's?' she prompted.

'Fantastic.' I put a hand each side of my face. 'I never realized I could look like that. So . . . so *different*.'

'Would you like to see the back,' she brandished a two-handled mirror now and came closer behind me.

The grey curls were all gone, and in their place was a sleek cap of silvery hair, feathered around a flushed and beaming face that suddenly didn't look very much like mine.

I would have paid her double or even treble what she asked quite happily. Instead, I gave Tina a hefty tip and booked another appointment for four weeks' time. Very short hair, she'd informed me, required regular cutting to keep it in shape.

'I don't think you'll have much trouble maintaining the style,' she said as she left, 'because without the perm your hair is nice and straight, though it's thick enough that it doesn't lie too flat to your head. You can fluff it up if you want to look a bit more funky and I think that will suit you, too.'

I went back inside, pausing before the mirror for another long, admiring look. It was getting late but I was far too hyped up to go to bed and, anyway, I wanted to play at dressing up.

Jeans. I pulled them from the bag. I hadn't worn a pair of jeans since I was a teenager, and I laughed in delight when I found I could fasten them without difficulty. The top I favoured was black, V-necked and made of some sort of soft cotton material but with a bit of a sheen to it. It was long enough to come down over my hips. I really needed boots for my feet, but I had none that were suitable, so my shoes would have to do — for now.

I'd never worn make-up and for the first time I regretted the lack. I told myself a smile would have to do. I needed a second opinion and I made my way down the stairs already laughing at the expected reaction when Greg opened the door.

'Bloody hell.' The words came out simultaneously and we stared at each other.

'You've had your hair cut.' We sounded like a pair of parrots, mimicking each other.

'You look great,' I said and meant it. I turned him around right there in the doorway, admiring the neatly trimmed hair. Greg looked like another person, almost handsome, in fact.

'And you,' he shook his head, 'look gorgeous and, I have to say it, I'm afraid, but I told you so. I know, I know,' he held up a hand, 'and you told me so. I absolutely accept that you were right. Cup of tea?'

'I suppose tea will have to do at this time of night.' I stepped inside. 'I'm just glad you didn't offer cocoa, because it really doesn't go with the hair.'

'And what about the clothes?' he called from the kitchen. 'Amazing what ditching the pleats has done for you. I'm wondering now if I can get away with a pair of jeans myself.' He poked his head round the door to ask, 'I'm not too old, am I?'

I laughed as I accepted my cup. 'You're not old at all,' I assured him, and we beamed at each other. I noticed neither of us made any attempt to touch the biscuits he'd arranged so nicely on a plate.

'I don't think number one on your list is beyond the realms of possibility, Mr Masters, with you looking like that.' I nodded approvingly, and suddenly found myself wondering if finding love again was beyond the realms of possibility for me. It was something I hadn't thought about in a very, very long time but suddenly anything seemed possible.

# 7

The comments when I arrived at work the next day came so thick and fast that while part of me was extremely gratified, another rather cynical part wondered what exactly everyone's opinion of my appearance must have been before.

'Jo, *Jo*, is that you?' The security guard on the front door did a double take, and added with great feeling, 'Bloody hell.'

'Have you seen Jo?' called the girl on the nearest check-out, and the question went like a ripple the length of the store, with every check-out operator pausing in the act of scanning goods to turn and give me the once over.

Denise stepped through the office door, did a double take and very nearly stepped out again. 'Good God,' she said, coming right in, 'it *is* you. I thought for a minute I was in the wrong office. Well,' she came over, took my hands and pulled me to my feet, 'no need to ask what you've been up to. Just look at you. Wow.'

I twirled round, eager for her honest opinion. It was one I knew I could count on from Denise, of all people. 'What do you think?' I said.

'You look,' she said with a delighted smile, 'absolutely amazing and also as if you've lost heaps of weight overnight. Now, how on earth did you manage that?'

'A combination of energetic decorating, no time to eat between meals, and clothes that fit, I think. I couldn't believe it when I could get into your old outfits and I can't thank you enough for thinking of me. If I'd had to buy a whole new wardrobe from scratch it would have cost me a small fortune.'

We had to postpone what might have been a lengthy discussion when the phones started ringing and work took over, but Denise insisted on treating me to lunch so that we could pick up where we left off.

'You look so young,' she marvelled over tuna and mayonnaise sandwiches. 'That haircut is marvellous and it's taken years off you.'

'Thank you,' I said modestly, resisting the urge to reach up and pat my short hair for the umpteenth time.

'I've never asked, and you can tell me to mind my own business, but exactly how old are you, Jo?'

'You should know,' I laughed, pointing out, 'it's right there in the file we hold on me.'

'And you know Cheapsmart has a policy of employing people of all ages,' she said seriously. 'The last thing we ever look at is a new applicant's age, so I'd hardly be checking out someone who's been working here for years, especially when she's a friend of mine.'

'How old did you think I was? You know, before all this,' I indicated the clothes and hair with a sweep of my hand.

'That's not fair,' she protested, and I knew she was right and eventually took pity on her.

'I'm less than ten years older than you, give or take a year,' I told her, and she let out a gasp before she could stifle it.

'You don't have to tell me, I know I looked as if I was about to collect my pension,' I said it before she felt obliged to.

For a long moment Denise was silent. Then she burst out, 'But *why*, Jo? You must have known you were doing yourself no favours — and I'm sorry if me saying that offends you — but what on earth were you thinking?'

I took a bite of my sandwich and chewed thoughtfully before I spoke. 'I wasn't thinking, Denise, I was surviving. My appearance was the last thing on my mind. I lived with an alcoholic husband, a young son and eventually a demanding mother. I was the only one in regular work, even when Petie grew up and should have been earning a wage, so there was never money to spare. It was a case of making do. I learned to home-perm my hair back when perms were in fashion and most of my clothes were originally my mother's. I stopped noticing the way I looked a very long time ago.'

'Oh, darling.' Denise put her hand on mine and looked as if she was going to burst into tears. 'I had no idea how bad things must have been for you.'

'How could you?' I asked. 'By the time we started working together it was just me and Petie.'

'And that wasn't always easy for you,' Denise remembered, and then shook herself, 'but now there's a whole new life waiting for the new woman you've become. Well done, Jo, you look amazing.'

'Can I buy you two young ladies a drink?' a masculine voice cut in, and we both looked up, ready to offer a quick rebuff to an unwelcome interloper.

'Greg,' I cried, unable to hide my pleasure at seeing him so unexpectedly. I turned quickly to Denise and offered the introduction, 'This is Greg Masters, Denise, my downstairs neighbour. Greg, this is Denise, my boss and very good friend.'

Denise held out her hand, 'Denise Mitchell, pleased to meet you, Greg. Handy with a paintbrush, so I've been told. You were honoured to be allowed to help; she wouldn't let us do a thing.'

'I *was* honoured, then,' Greg laughed. 'Now what about those drinks?'

'It'll have to be another time.' I looked regretfully at my watch. 'It's time for us to be getting back.'

'That's the drawback of sharing lunch with your boss,' Denise told him, getting to her feet and shrugging a lightweight jacket on. 'It was nice to meet you, Greg.'

'Likewise,' he said, and then turning to me, he went on, 'I popped into the adult education office this morning and picked up details of cake decorating courses they're going to be running. I'll let you have a look later. Have a good afternoon.'

Denise barely made it outside before she burst out, 'Well, you're a dark horse.'

I stared at her. 'What on earth do you mean?'

'From somewhere I got the impression he was a scruffy old man, and now I find out he's actually neither of those things. In fact, he's actually a very nice-looking and relatively young man.'

'Is he?' I was totally taken aback. Granted he had scrubbed up well, but nice-looking?

'Don't play the innocent with me,' she

scoffed. 'He really likes you and if I'm not mistaken, you really like him.'

'Well, of *course* we like each other. Friends do, Denise, but don't start seeing something that isn't there, or I shall think you're as bad as old Edna Gutheridge and she's telling everyone who will listen that we're having a red-hot affair.'

'And you're not?' Denise sounded disappointed and I gave her a little push and told her, 'Just stop it.'

We walked on arm in arm, but I knew she wasn't going to leave it there, and I was right.

'Cake decorating courses?'

'Just one of the things on my list of things to do,' I told her airily, refusing to elaborate or to add that Greg was interested in going as well. I had a feeling I'd never hear the end of it.

A distraction was accomplished by bringing the conversation round to make-up. Not that I had any intention of plastering my face, but I thought a sweep of mascara and a touch of lipstick might not go amiss and even complement the new me. The rest of the walk back to work was spent discussing the merits of this brand or that.

I was pleased with what had been accomplished so far, and during the afternoon I sneaked a quick peep at my list, suddenly keen to tick a few more things off. Realizing that some of the items might take a while, I concentrated on the couple of things that could be accomplished quickly.

Like the ear piercing, I stabbed the point of my pen at number nine and decided to get it done on Saturday morning. Number ten drew my eye, being next in line, and I wondered where on earth I would find details of a reputable clairvoyant.

I was perusing the Yellow Pages that evening at home, when there was the knock at the door, which I'd been expecting. I jumped up, pleased that at least Greg and I would be making a start on number three if his cake decorating courses turned out to be suitable for a couple of beginners.

I threw open the door with a flourish, but it wasn't Greg on the step.

'Petie,' I cried, delighted to find myself wrapped in a bear hug from the son who had seemed to have grown in stature and confidence over just a couple of years.

'I'm sorry it's been so long,' he apologized, 'but you know what it's like.'

For once I could agree with the latter and mean it, realizing with a pang that I'd been so busy myself I'd hardly noticed the passing of time. Normally, I would have been fretting that Petie hadn't visited for a while, though it was some time since I'd worried about what he might be getting up to. A steady job working with a man he looked up to had finally changed the tearaway boy into a responsible adult. These days, like me, he was just very busy getting on with his life.

'Wow, look at this place — and look at you. What on earth have you been doing to yourself, Mum?' He held me at arm's length and stared at me as if he couldn't believe his eyes.

'Don't you like it?' I suddenly felt silly. Like a child who'd been caught raiding a dressing-up box. I was still the old insecure me inside, after all, and realized with a pang that it was going to take more than a change of clothes and a haircut to change my life and the way I felt about myself.

'Like it?' Petie said, adjusted his glasses for another closer look, and then said again louder, so that I flinched, '*like* it? I don't like it, Mum, I *love* it, you look fabulous.'

'Really?'

'Really. Surely you don't even have to ask? Just look at yourself in the mirror there.'

The door to the flat still stood open and we both turned at the sound of a tentative tap. Greg stood on the threshold, clasping a handful of papers and looking tentatively at the pair of us.

'I'm sorry, I'm intruding,' he began to turn away, 'I'll call back later.'

I tutted and called him back. 'Don't be silly, come on in and meet my son. This is Peter.'

Greg came forward then, still looking a little uncertain, but he put out his hand, 'I'm Greg.'

'No introduction necessary,' Petie assured him. 'I know all about you.'

We both stared at him, mystified.

'Yes, you're obviously the man my mother is having a *torrid affair* with. I've heard all about it.' Petie raised his voice and his eyebrows, and with a nod he indicated the open doorway and we could all see the slight movement beyond of a bright yellow duster. Then he closed the door and snorted with derisive laughter, which he quickly stifled, and we all giggled our way to the kitchen.

'You're so naughty, Petie. Edna really shouldn't be encouraged,' I scolded.

'Oh, Mum, you know she doesn't need encouraging. What she doesn't know she just makes up.' Petie turned to Greg. 'I expect I have you to thank for the way Mum's decorating is moving along. I'm not sure if you had a hand in her new look, too, but everything looks great, including Mum. What have you got there?'

I got on with making the tea, leaving Greg to explain about the classes, about his own circumstances and how we had become friends, encouraging each other to step out of our own particular comfort zone and make some changes for the better to our lives.

'You sound as if you've had a hard time of it, Greg,' Petie's tone was sympathetic, and he added, 'I know my Mum has, first with my Dad and his problems, and then with me and mine. Do you have any children, Greg?'

'Sadly, no, and it's something I've always regretted.'

'We can be a blessing and a curse,' Petie said ruefully. 'My Mum's grey hair can largely be put down to me, I'm afraid.'

'But she wouldn't be without you for the world,' Greg insisted, without hesitation, 'and she'll want to spend some time with you now, so I shall leave these leaflets, Jo, for you to read at your leisure. We can decide another time whether any of the courses are what we're looking for.'

With that, he drank his tea in one go and got up to leave, despite both Petie and I assuring him he was very welcome to stay.

'Nice guy,' was Petie's comment when the front door had closed behind him. 'I'm glad you have a friend like that close by because, selfishly, it makes me feel better about not getting round as often as I should.'

'And I'm glad you're not trying to make more out of it than friendship, because there really is nothing more between us.'

'Don't you think I would know immediately if there was?' Petie laughed, and patted my hand in an affectionate gesture. 'You've always been totally transparent and honest as the day is long. Not that I'd be unhappy if you found love again, because you, of all people, deserve to be happy.'

'Oh, Petie,' I felt my eyes begin to brim with silly tears, 'what a lovely thing to say.'

'Well, not all men are like my Dad, you know.'

We drank our tea companionably, discussed my list in detail, with Petie making various suggestions. Then Petie checked on the decorating already accomplished and the work in progress on the bedroom.

When he encouraged me to put the kettle on again, the suspicions I had about the real reason for his visit grew and spread like wildfire, but I said nothing until we were seated once more at the table. Then I could contain myself no longer.

'Petie,' I said, looking straight at him, 'have you got something you want to tell me?'

He laughed awkwardly. 'How do you do that, Mum, am I transparent, too?'

'You're not in trouble, are you, Petie?' I hated even to say it, but I really couldn't help myself. The past and all its troubles could not be ignored. 'You would tell me if you were?'

'I'm not,' he said hastily, and relief flooded though me, until he added, 'Well, not exactly.'

I literally felt the blood drain from my face and an icy hand squeeze my heart so tightly that I found it difficult to breathe.

'Don't look like that,' he pleaded, 'it's nothing for you to worry about.'

The way he said it just convinced me all the more that I had every reason to be concerned and I insisted, 'Just tell me what it is and then I can be the judge.'

'I've sort of got a girlfriend,' he said sheepishly, 'I've been seeing her for a while.'

I almost laughed out loud and said, 'A girlfriend — is that all?' But that wasn't all. I knew my son and there was more to it than that for him to be making such a pig's breakfast out of telling me about it.

'And?'

'And she's pregnant?' he said flatly.

# 8

The silence that lay between Petie and me was almost tangible. He was looking at me defiantly, in much the same way he had always used to do when he had done something he knew I would disapprove of, and he was clearly waiting for me to voice that disapproval.

I didn't know what to say — and it wasn't very often I was lost for words. In the end two words escaped involuntarily. 'Oh, Petie,' I said.

'You think I messed up again, don't you?' he accused and it was all I could do not to agree.

Eventually, I said, 'What do you think?'

'You always said I was the best thing that happened to you. Don't you think this might be the best thing that's happened to me?'

I sidestepped giving a direct answer and kept my hands firmly in my lap in case I threw them up with the sheer horror of it all. 'I think only you can possibly know the answer to that. Do you love — ?'

'Lizzie,' he put in helpfully. 'Her name is Lizzie.'

'Lizzie.' The name was unfamiliar on my tongue, but then it would be since the girl was obviously a complete stranger to me. 'Do you?'

'I think I do, yes.'

It seemed like a pretty lukewarm thing to say about the mother of your unborn child. He *thought* he loved her, but I knew I should be used to this scenario given the job that I did. In the Human Resources department at Cheapsmart girls coming in to tell us they were pregnant and the father had done a runner, or wasn't quite ready to commit to them and the baby was practically an everyday occurrence.

The fact that this time it involved my son and — I swallowed deeply at the thought — my grandchild, well, that put a whole different slant on things. I could tell myself I wasn't going to get involved but, like the poor child, I already was.

'And how does she ... Lizzie ... feel about this? How does she feel about you?'

'Well, that's the thing, you see, I don't really know.'

'You haven't talked about it?' I said, quite mildly, when what I wanted to say quite forcefully was: you haven't talked about feelings or the future, yet you've made love and presumably slept in one another's arms.

'Lizzie doesn't want me to feel under any pressure to make a decision that may not be right for me.'

'What about what's right for Lizzie,' I asked, 'and the baby?'

'We don't want to stay together just for the baby.'

Common sense told me they were absolutely right, but I wasn't actually thinking with my head at that moment. This wasn't what I had imagined for Petie or for my first grandchild, especially since Petie had turned his life around and become the man I had always hoped he might one day be.

All those years of protecting him from the worst of his father's alcoholism, the constantly giving in to Jack's demands for both money and sex, so that Petie wouldn't see the resulting fury if I didn't. All those years of sleepless nights, the fretting and worrying after both Jack and my mother were gone, as I fought, sometimes fruitlessly, to keep Petie on the straight and narrow — and just when I thought I had nothing else to worry about he'd come up with something I hadn't even thought of. It was all I could do not to break down and weep right in front of my son.

'You feel as if I've let you down again, don't you?' Petie obviously knew me too well, and denials and protestations would fool neither one of us.

I tried to explain. 'I always tried to take care of everything for you, but in the end even I had to give you a push out into the world and allow you to take responsibility for your own choices and mistakes. I wish there was some way I could help with this but, once again, I have to say you're on your own. It hurts me to say that because this is, after all, my first grandchild we're talking about. I have to leave it to you and Lizzie to do what you think is best for both of you, and for the child. Now I've said that, I'm sure you know without me saying it, that I will always be here for you one hundred per cent, and that I trust you to do the right thing — whatever that is.'

'Thanks, Mum.' He took his glasses off and polished the lens on the sleeve of his sweater and I could swear I saw the glitter of tears in his eyes.

In that moment he looked more like my little boy than the big strapping man he actually was and I could see that he was scared. We hugged for a long time as he left and he kissed me so tenderly that it was hard for me to hold back the tears. I stood looking down over the banister long after I heard the outside door close behind him and I had never felt so lonely in all of my life.

I needed a friend in that moment as I never had before, and it was getting late, far too late to be knocking at anyone's door, but my feet seemed to have developed a mind of their own and they carried me step by step to Greg's door. Once there, I hesitated no longer and used the knocker with confidence.

He took so long to answer the door that I began to think he was out. I had already turned to make my way disconsolately back up the stairs when I heard the Yale lock turn. Greg stood there in Jack's old navy towelling robe, his new haircut all mussed. I knew I had got him out of bed, but he still smiled when he saw it was me knocking at his door.

'You didn't have to make a decision about the cake decorating class tonight, Jo,' he joked, 'tomorrow would have done just as well.' Then he must have seen the look on my face and he became serious in a minute. 'What is it?' he asked. 'What's happened?'

I don't know how, one minute we were standing face to face and the next I was in his arms and crying my heart out on his broad shoulder. Somehow, with very little apparent effort, he managed to get us both through the door and closed it behind us.

'Jo, oh, Jo, what is it, my dear?'

He smoothed my short hair and patted my

back as if I were a wailing infant. When my sobs had subsided to a hiccoughing halt, he pressed me into an armchair, handed me a clean hanky and went to put the kettle on, rattling about with cups and saucers and giving me time to become composed again.

With the tray between us, he asked, 'Do you want to talk about it? Only don't feel that you have to. We can just sit quietly while we drink our tea, if that's what you want.'

I managed a watery smile and told him, 'You're a good friend, Greg, one of the best.'

'That's nice to hear, and it's how I feel about you, too.'

For a little while we sat in companionable silence, sipping our tea, but I knew I had come here to Greg for a reason and that reason was to talk — and soon it all came tumbling out.

He heard me out, without interruption, removing the sodden handkerchief from my grasp and handing me a clean one when the tears began to fall again.

'What is it you're so afraid of, Jo?' he asked me, and I stared at him, searching for an answer.

'Anything and everything,' I admitted at last and, counting on my fingers, I went on, 'that the pressure will be too much for him and he'll go back to his wild ways, that this

108

Lizzie will expect him to marry her and it won't be what he wants, that she won't want him to marry her but marrying her will be what he wants, that she won't want him at all once she's had his child, and most of all that because of any decision they make I won't be part of my own grandchild's life.' I was out of breath by the time I got to the end.

'What can you do about any of that?'

'We-ll,' I dragged out the word, 'nothing, I suppose, except to be there for Petie — for them both if I'm allowed — and leave them to make their own decisions.' I scowled at Greg, 'But it's hard to stand back when your own flesh and blood is involved.'

'I can imagine it is,' Greg said softly. 'I've heard that you never stop worrying about your children, no matter how old they are, but if you bring them up to be responsible adults, surely you have to trust them to do the right thing.'

'I suppose they have to learn from their mistakes, just as we did, but they just seem to jump right in without a thought these days,' I mused. 'I remember Denise going through all of this when her daughter Bobbi got pregnant — she hadn't long been at university and her boyfriend was a complete nightmare at the time.'

'What happened?' Greg sounded as if he really cared.

'Bobbi is a qualified nurse now, her boyfriend turned his life around and they eventually married, their little girl is adorable, but one happy ending doesn't mean they'll all turn out that way, Greg.'

'Your son is a fine young man, Jo. You've done a great job with him. I know you haven't met this Lizzie yet, but I'm sure she can't be all bad — not if Peter loves her. Try letting go and trusting them to do what's best — what's best for them and for the baby — and yes, I do know that's easy for me to say.'

I heaved a huge sigh. All the tension went out of me at what almost amounted to being given permission not to get involved in my son's problems, leaving me so tired I could have fallen asleep right then and there. 'How did you get to be so wise?' I demanded with a little laugh.

'Like all non-parents, I'm great on the theory side of bringing up kids.' He grinned back at me.

I stood up. 'Thank you, thank you, and I'm really sorry I got you out of bed.'

'It was my pleasure, and even more so to know you would have done exactly the same for me.'

'I think I will sleep now,' I said as I left, and

sure enough I did, right through the night.

Of course, I told Denise all about it next day because she, of all people, would understand exactly how I was feeling. She was suitably horrified on my account, realizing as I had that the circumstances weren't ideal and the relationship precarious in its newness.

'Greg's right, though, isn't he?' she asked. 'In the end they will make their own decisions regardless of your wishes or concerns, and a new baby in the family is hardly the end of the world. As you can plainly see from what happened in my family. How did you leave it with Petie?'

'Basically, I had already said to him what both you and Greg have said to me, that it's up to him and this . . . this Lizzie . . . to decide what's best for them and for the baby, too. He knows where I am if he needs me, Denise, but it's bloody hard just to leave them to get on with it, isn't it?'

She nodded sympathetically, and then changing the subject determinedly, she suggested, 'Why don't we go shopping on Saturday? We haven't done that in ages. We'll have a great time and it'll take your mind off a situation you can't do anything about. Petie will tell you what's happening, I'm sure, the very minute he knows what's happening himself.'

'Yes,' I could feel myself brightening at the thought, 'and I'll get a shift on with the bedroom this week, so that anything new I might buy can go straight into my own wardrobe in my own room.'

'You can have supper at mine after the shopping trip, too. I won't take no for an answer. We might even persuade Adam to cook for us. He's getting to be quite a dab hand in the kitchen these days — reckons it helps him to unwind.'

★　★　★

In a rush of renewed enthusiasm, I set to the minute I got home. Before long Greg joined me and two rollers certainly covered my walls more quickly than one. He was encouraging about the shopping trip, too, when we discussed my and Denise's plans over the pizza we had delivered once we'd decided that neither of us felt like cooking.

'It'll be nice for you to choose clothes to suit your own taste, won't it?' he enthused. 'Denise's generosity gave you the opportunity to try clothes more in keeping with the new you, but now you'll be able to develop your own style.'

Greg's confidence in my ability to do just that made me feel certain he was right, and I really started to look forward to the kind of trip to the shops that I had previously avoided like the plague.

We took a last look at a bedroom that looked strange and beautiful to me. Gone was the heavily flowered paper to make way for clean walls in a gorgeous blush pink.

'I can get the paintwork done tomorrow,' Greg offered, adding, 'two coats if I get the first one on early enough.'

I was sorely tempted to accept with alacrity but felt guilty about taking up all of his time, and, when he questioned my hesitation, I admitted as much.

'We're friends,' he reminded me, 'and friends help each other out.'

'And I'm helping you by doing what exactly?' I questioned.

'Oh, well,' he said, 'if you're getting a guilty conscience you could make your mind up about which class we're going to join for the cake decorating and I'll get us booked in. It's about time I crossed something else off my list and I freely confess I haven't got the nerve to go to something like that alone. We both know it'll be full of women.'

I laughed at the fearful look on his face, and reminded him, 'I'm a woman, or don't I count?'

'You're a friend and that makes you

different. I'm not expecting anyone to jump on me or anything, but I'll just feel safer if you're with me.'

'Go on then. I'll admit it's not much fun walking into any of these sort of things alone anyway. People have a way of looking at you as if you were an alien that just landed. You can choose which course will suit us best; just make sure it's in the evening and that it's not too advanced.'

'Once the paintwork is done, I'll give you a hand to get the bed back up and the furniture in place.' Greg changed the subject with a speed that might have been confusing, but I caught up with him quite easily.

'I thought I might get a new bed,' I said suddenly, although I hadn't, at least not until that very moment, 'but will it take ages to come?'

'There are shops that deliver the same day,' he pointed out helpfully, adding, 'I could pick you up in your lunch break tomorrow so that you can check a couple out. What about the carpet?'

We both eyed it doubtfully. There was no escaping the fact it had seen better days. I was tempted, but was beginning to feel a bit overwhelmed and very conscious that I would have to depend on Greg's help to get that sorted, too, *and* there was just no way the whole thing could be achieved by the end of the week.

I said as much, and trying to inject some enthusiasm into my tone, went on, 'I can put rugs down as I did in the hall. It will be fine, but I'll be glad of your help with getting the bed ordered. It'll be great to see the back of that old thing.'

I wasn't sure whether to be grateful or disappointed when he didn't pursue the matter and couldn't believe how contrary I was becoming.

★ ★ ★

'He was there with his paintbrush before I even left for work,' I told Denise. 'I insisted on making him breakfast and it was the strangest feeling to be sharing toast with a man again.'

'Quite nice, I would imagine.' Denise looked up from some forms she was perusing to say, 'The state of some of these job applications has to be seen to be believed. You'd think some of them didn't know what a full stop was and as for the spelling . . . It was one of the things I loved most when Adam first moved in with me, that and sleeping with someone again — and I'm not talking about the sex. Well,' she went on with a smile, 'of course, I love that too, it goes without saying but just sleeping in someone's arms again was so lovely.'

'I'll take your word for it,' I said drily, very conscious of just how many years had passed since I'd shared a bed with anyone or had breakfast with a man who wasn't Petie. 'Anyway, I'm skipping lunch today to go and choose a new bed. Greg is picking me up — because he has a car and I don't — and because he's a friend, before you ask or hint at anything more.'

'I believe you, and I wasn't going to.' Denise went back to the application forms and I could hear her tutting clear across the office.

It wasn't until she looked up and said, 'Oh, hello, Greg, come on in,' that I realized the whole morning had slipped by almost unnoticed.

'Oh, I'm sorry,' I said, adding one last figure to a spreadsheet and feeling cross with myself for not being ready and waiting when he was giving up even more of his time for me, 'I meant to be out in the car park waiting.' I turned in my chair, adding, 'I won't be more than a minute.'

I couldn't help being pleased to notice he had changed out of his paint-spattered overalls into blue jeans and a lighter blue polo shirt, but refraining from comment I stood up and reached for my jacket instead.

'We shouldn't be long,' I told Denise, 'and I'll get those interview invites out as soon as I get back.'

'Take your time,' she insisted, 'it'll make up for some of the lunch breaks you've worked through, and go for something snazzy, like king-sized or round.'

'She was joking,' I told Greg, as we made our way through the shop, and then felt I had to ask, 'but they don't really make round beds, do they? How on earth would you make the sheets fit?'

'I'm sure they do,' he laughed, probably amused at my shocked expression, 'for film stars and footballers, and they would definitely be able to buy sheets especially made to fit.'

Holding open the door of a very smart Vauxhall Vectra in gleaming silver, he waited until I was comfortably settled before closing it and going round to the driver's side.

'Do we know where we're going?' I asked as he climbed in. 'Shouldn't we have checked the Yellow Pages or something?'

'There's a place in Kinton, according to the adverts on the radio, so I thought we'd try there as it's fairly close.'

'It is good of you to take me like this.'

'It's my pleasure.' Greg's voice was firm and I relaxed back into the seat.

He was right about the shop; we were there in no time. He was right about the same day deliveries, too.

'You and your husband can be sleeping in the bed of your choice by tonight,' the young lady assistant assured me.

I glanced at Greg and saw his mouth twitch, though he pulled it straight in a moment. I didn't have the heart to correct the girl and cause her to be embarrassed and to start speculating about what exactly our relationship was. I regretted that decision when she had us both testing the beds by lying on them side by side, but Greg got right into the part, even bouncing up and down and advising me to, 'go for one with drawers for all those new clothes you're going to buy.'

'Crumbs, isn't he understanding?' the girl looked astonished. 'My boyfriend is always telling me I have far too many and certainly no room for more.'

Greg looked so smug that I almost burst out laughing, especially when he told her in all seriousness, 'I always say a lady can never have too many clothes and when they say they have nothing to wear it's no more than the truth.'

I left them talking, probably about what a perfect husband he must be, and decided on my choice of bed without help from either of them. A normal double-sized, oblong divan, with drawers and a nice padded headboard in a deep rose pink. I could imagine it in pride of place in my newly decorated bedroom, and best of all, it would hide most of the shabby carpet.

The order was placed, and a time for delivery arranged with Greg, who assured me he would be there, so not to worry about rushing home from work.

Then Greg ruined the whole illusion of us as the happily married couple by saying, quite innocently, as we took our leave of the beaming assistant, 'You've been really helpful. I'll certainly come here when I'm ready to replace my bed.'

What made it even funnier was that he didn't even realize what he'd said until he was outside in the car park and realized I was doubled up with laughter.

'She probably just thinks I snore and, being the perfect husband, I sleep in a separate room so that you get a good night's rest,' he informed me with a self-satisfied smirk.

'She probably does,' I agreed, and found myself thinking that he was the kind of man who would actually do just that. After all, he had given up just about everything to nurse his sick wife.

He was the kind of man I should have married all those years ago but, of course, he wouldn't have been my type then, any more than he was my type now. I couldn't help thinking what a pity that was.

# 9

I couldn't wait to get home after work to see if the new bed had really been delivered as promised. I paused only long enough to pick up a couple of chicken breasts from the chilled meat cabinet, a packet of savoury rice and some of that sweet and sour sauce in a jar. Cooking something for Greg's supper was the least I could do, I'd decided, and even I couldn't go far wrong with something as simple as that.

On reflection, I felt a little ashamed that my culinary skills had sunk so low and wondered what had happened to that dab-hand-in-the-kitchen woman who could work miracles with half a pound of mince and a couple of dented tins from the reduced price shelves in the supermarket. It was only recalling Greg saying that company was more important than the food that stopped me from giving up on the idea of cooking at all and resorting to fish and chips or some other takeaway again.

'You've been busy, I could smell the fresh paint from halfway up the stairs,' I was saying as I let myself in and hurried eagerly towards the open bedroom door. I came to an abrupt halt on the threshold, said, 'Oh,' dropped the bags I was carrying and clapped my hands to my face.

Greg looked up from where he was kneeling in the corner of the room. He had a mouthful of tacks and a raised hammer in his hand.

'I was trying to finish this before you got back,' he sounded cross with himself, even allowing for the tacks in his teeth and then, when I remained silent, he looked anxious and removing them from his mouth he said flatly, 'You don't like it, do you?'

'But it's a new carpet, Greg, a *new carpet*. We only ordered a bed. How did it happen? Where did you get it from so quickly and what happened to the old one?'

'Well, I took it to the tip . . . erm, recycling centre with the old bed . . . was that all right? You didn't want to keep it for anything did you? And I had to guess at the colour you might want, so I tried to match it to the new headboard from memory. I wanted it to be a surprise, but you hate it, don't you? I'm so sorry, I think I got a bit carried away.'

He looked beside himself when I burst into noisy tears, and I had to hasten to tell him, 'I love it, Greg. I can't begin to tell you how much. No one has ever done anything like that for me in my life, but how did you do it all so quickly — and all the painting, too. It looks gorgeous, far better than I could ever have imagined.'

'I'm afraid I haven't managed to put the bed together yet, as you can see, but that won't take long. The carpet was just an off-cut, and you can bring those away from the store with you. It was just lucky they had a piece to fit and in the right sort of colour. I picked it up right after I dropped you off and, because I started so early this morning I'd already got the two coats of paint on the woodwork before I collected you at lunchtime, which gave the second coat time to dry, but you don't want to hear about all of that, do you?'

'Oh, I do,' I assured him, 'I want to hear every little detail, but first I'm going to throw this food together and make something resembling a meal. I'm also going to promise to take you out for a proper meal at a decent restaurant in the very near future. Thank you, Greg. Thank you *so* much.'

★ ★ ★

'And I ended up hugging him and embarrassed us both,' I told Denise over coffee and muffins, which was the starting point for every shopping trip we ever went on.

'What a *lovely* man,' she exclaimed for the umpteenth time, since we'd done nothing *but* discuss his kindness over what had remained of the working week. 'I liked him straight away, you know, and I'm a pretty good judge of character.' She looked smug as she went on, 'You couldn't stand him for ages, as I recall.'

'You wouldn't have been impressed, either,' I defended my early impression of Greg, reminding her, 'he was a real old scruff-bag. I've seen smarter tramps than he used to be, honestly. Did I tell you about the row we had when we tried telling each other a few home truths about the way we both looked?'

We were off, then, laughing about those 'home truths' and the outraged reaction we'd had to them but, as I recalled, it hadn't been funny at the time and had almost finished what was still a fairly new friendship with my downstairs neighbour for good.

'Do you think it would be all right for me to buy him a sweater or something without it being misconstrued?' I mused, feeling the urge to do *something* after all Greg had done for me.

'If he could buy and fit your bedroom carpet without that being misconstrued,' Denise retorted, 'I should think a sweater would be absolutely fine.' Then she spoiled it by adding, 'Are you quite sure there's no chance of you two, you know . . . ' she did have the grace to hesitate before blundering on, 'getting together as *more* than friends?'

I silenced her with a look, and an emphatic, 'No, no chance. I mean it, Denise, it's just never going to happen.'

'OK,' she shrugged, 'I only asked. Keep your lovely new hair on.'

'He is looking for a lady, though, so if you can think of anybody suitable . . . '

'I'll give it some thought,' she promised, and, taking a bite of her cherry and almond muffin, murmured with her mouth full, 'mmm, this is delicious. How's yours?'

Mine was vanilla and white chocolate. I showed my appreciation by closing my eyes and uttering, 'Mmmm-*mmm*,' so loudly that we both laughed.

'Now,' said Denise in a business-like tone, 'it's about time you crossed a few more things off that list of yours. OK, I know the makeover and the decorating are still work-in-progress, but you need to move along and this is for your next project.' She handed me a business card, saying, 'and I've already paid for the first six, so don't even think about arguing or trying to bottle out.'

I stared first at her and then at the card.

'Driving lessons? Oh, Denise, I don't think I'm ready for something as complicated as that. I'm not seventeen any more, you know.'

'Just as well,' she said sternly, 'there are quite enough youngsters on the road, so we need to even it out a bit. This chap taught Bobbi when she was at home on maternity leave and, as you know, she passed her test first time.'

'Oh, no pressure then,' I muttered, putting the card in my purse and cursing a list of items that had seemed all too achievable in the comfort of my own sitting room, especially with Greg egging me on. In the cold hard light of day, I was beginning to regret ever starting. Or was I?

True, it hadn't always been easy, and sometimes I'd almost had to be dragged kicking and screaming just a few steps forward towards a new me, but I liked the person I saw in the mirror each day now and, despite the upheaval, my home was finally becoming the haven I had always longed for. Somewhere to relax and unwind, light, bright and uncluttered, there was little left to remind me of the difficult days of the past.

'I'll do it,' I said firmly, 'I'll book the lessons first thing on Monday morning and thank you.'

Denise clapped her hands. 'Bravo,' she

crowed, and then she lifted her coffee cup, clinked it to mine and said, 'making that list has certainly led to you making a change for the better to your life.'

'A change for the better,' I nodded, 'I like the sound of that. What a pity I didn't do it sooner.'

'None of that,' Denise insisted as we left the coffee shop arm in arm. 'You can only do these things when the time is right. Look at me.'

I did, and she looked amazing, which I didn't hesitate to say.

' 'But I struggled for more than a year after Rob died before I felt ready to reinvent myself,' she pointed out. 'You can only do it when it feels right. I was lucky because I had a daughter whose clothes and make-up I could experiment with in the privacy of my own home. I know you've had the benefit of some of mine recently, but now we're going to find out what really suits you and I can't wait.'

I think I got a bit carried away because I'm sure the ear piercing was all my idea, telling myself and Denise there was no time like the present. I winced at the crunch — real or imagined — as the studs were fired into my lobes but then I immediately felt elated at another item being erased from my list and couldn't help but be impressed with my own bravery. I couldn't wait to show Greg the neat little gold studs adorning my ears.

Fiddling with make-up samples was Denise's idea. I'd never been one for 'putting a face on' and complained I'd never have the time anyway, though I wasn't averse to a dab of nail varnish.

'All that powdering and preening is far too much like hard work,' I screwed up my nose, 'and I'm sure it won't suit me anyway.'

I should have just kept my mouth shut and left Denise to try the samples because the assistant obviously saw me as a challenge. She was out from behind the counter and had swept me up onto a stool before you could say blusher and wooshed a little cape around my shoulders before I realized what was happening.

'Do you mind?' she asked, and when I opened my mouth to say yes, she swiped such generous amounts of cleansing lotion all over my face that I had to shut it again quite swiftly.

'We'll keep it simple,' she said, smiling from behind a mask of make-up that made her look like a beautiful porcelain doll.

*She* could get away with it, I told myself, glowering at Denise who didn't even try to hide a satisfied smirk, after trying and failing for years in her efforts to get me to try even as much as a dab of lipstick.

Cleansed, toned and moisturised, it seemed I was ready for the next step and I again opened my mouth to protest, only to almost swallow the soft bristles of an enormous brush.

'Just sweep a touch of bronzer right over your face and neck,' the girl — Olivia, according to her badge — advised, continuing the information that it would, 'even out my skin tone and hide any blemishes.'

Yes, but what about the wrinkles was the question hovering on the end of my tongue and the protestation, and I don't want to look as if I've been lying on a sun bed, was close behind it. In the end I just gave up and let her get on with it, reminding myself there was a packet of wet wipes in my bag. They would soon obliterate all traces of Olivia's handiwork so no harm was being done.

Denise had wandered away to try some perfume samples and I could see her out of the corner of my newly made-up eye making her way back, just as the cape was whipped from my shoulders with a flourish and a very satisfied, 'There you are,' from Olivia.

Denise stopped dead and stared at me open-mouthed. 'Oh, Jo,' she said finally, 'you look beautiful.'

'Don't sound so surprised,' I grumped peevishly, 'and it *is* only a bit of make-up.'

Denise wasn't even listening to me. 'Whatever products you've used on Jo today, we're buying,' she told Olivia, who looked absolutely delighted.

I started to protest, convinced it would cost and arm and at least a couple of legs, but my mouth snapped shut when a mirror was thrust in front of me and for once in my life I was speechless.

'Well, what do you think?' Denise demanded impatiently.

'I look . . . different,' I managed at last, 'but not really made up at all.' I turned to Olivia in amazement. 'How did you do it? And more to the point, how do *I* do it?'

'With a good skincare routine and a light touch with very little in the way of make-up.' The girl was smiling, obviously thrilled to see my pleasure. 'We'll go through it step by step, but you will find with practice that it actually takes very little time to achieve a similar result.'

'And to think all these years I've made do with soap and water,' I marvelled to Denise as we finally left the store and Olivia behind, with her instructions ringing in my ears, a depleted purse and a deceptively light carrier bag.

'I doubt that in the past you had the time or money to spend on yourself, did you?' Denise asked, and then went on to point out, kindly I thought, 'You've always been an attractive woman, Jo, and now you're just learning to make the best of yourself.'

I looked at my reflection in the windows as we passed, and wondered what had happened to that old woman I had once seen looking back at me — and it wasn't even all that long ago. It was all I could do not to give a little hop, skip and a jump of pure joy.

Even buying clothes was a whole new experience for me, since it had always been a chore and not something I'd ever found any pleasure in. The sales that were on everywhere made it easy to justify the additional expense and, as Denise so rightly said, we'd be doing our bit for the economy and for ourselves.

It would have been easy to get carried away, to buy ten sets of new underwear instead of two, shoes in every colour with handbags to match, not to mention trousers, skirts, tops and dresses that made me look and feel younger by the minute. Under Denise's guidance, however, I restrained myself and settled on a few basics that I could build on over time, and enjoyed the unusual — for me — feel of carrier bag handles cutting into my fingers.

Somewhere along the way we managed to fit in delicious panini, which we shared, reminding ourselves that if we ate too much we'd have no room for the supper Adam had offered to prepare.

'You have about half an hour before it's ready,' he greeted us when we finally arrived at Denise's house, 'so why don't you put your feet up and have a glass of wine. You look as if you've earned it,' he added, with a smiling nod at the numerous bags Denise had insisted I bring in so that we could enthuse again over the contents.

'Well,' Denise urged me towards the stairs, 'I think you should put on something new. Adam would love to see the new you, wouldn't you, darling?'

'I can't wait,' he said immediately, but added very sweetly I thought, 'though there wasn't actually anything wrong with the old Jo as far as I was concerned.'

'He probably thought there was nothing wrong with the old me either,' Denise smiled fondly, 'and he'd be right, but I'm all in favour of giving nature a hand if it makes you feel better about yourself and I certainly do, I don't know about you?'

I nodded, 'I never thought I'd say it, but I finally like my life and I like the person I see in the mirror. I can't wait to get up in the morning because there's so much going on. It's amazing. My only worry is . . . '

'Petie,' Denise finished for me, adding, 'I know. God, don't I know after the problems I had with Bobbi and Jason, *and* my mother.'

We both grew silent as we remembered the way they had all moved in and taken over Denise's house, not to mention her life, effectively preventing her from getting on with her own when she'd finally found herself ready to do so.

'You can offer advice and encouragement, Jo, but that's really all you can do. Petie is an adult now and in the end he will do what he thinks is the right thing, and knowing Petie these days, I'm sure it will be. Anyway,' she went on briskly, 'I'm going down to see if Adam needs a hand. Get dressed up and then come down when you're ready and surprise us.'

Standing in the room that used to be Bobbi's, I felt ridiculously excited for a woman in her fifties as I dipped into the bags and selected items of clothing I thought would look good together. It was years since I'd dressed up and I loved the newness of the garments. The panelled skirt in shades of blue slipped easily over my slimmed-down hips, and put with a white V-neck short-sleeved cardigan with a bit of lace detail to the sleeves and shoulders, which I used on its own as a top, I couldn't deny it made a stunning outfit.

Plain white sling-back shoes with a bit of a heel were the final touch, and I swivelled and turned, smiling at my reflection, and feeling so happy I thought I would burst. Looking back at me was the woman I'd always wanted to be, confident, happy and in charge of her own destiny, a woman for whom good things would surely happen.

'Are you ready yet?' Adam called up. 'Only, the suspense is killing me and I'm about ready to dish up.'

'I'm just coming,' I said, and stopping only to retouch my lips with coral and to ruffle my hair slightly with my fingertips, I straightened my back, gave a brisk nod to the woman in the mirror and made my way from the room.

'Oh. My. God.' Denise was standing in the hall and, looking up, she clapped a hand to her mouth.

'Well, would you look at that lady,' Adam came to stand beside his wife and went on. 'I don't know exactly what you've done to yourself, Jo, but you look amazing. I feel that I should have offered to take you both out for a meal now that you're all dressed up with nowhere to go.'

'We'll light some candles, drink some

champagne,' said Denise, looking at me and shaking her head, 'and celebrate a new start for my best and very gorgeous friend.'

I laughed a little nervously, and pleaded, 'Would you both stop looking at me like that, and you don't have to make a fuss, it's just a few new clothes.'

'A bit more than that,' Denise insisted, as we bustled backwards and forwards between kitchen and dining room while Adam dished up, 'because it's not only your appearance that's changed, is it?'

'No, I admitted, touching the lighted taper to the candles we'd added to the table, 'it's not. I feel like a completely different person, inside and out, and it's great.'

Right on cue, Adam appeared in the doorway and popped the cork on a bottle of champagne. When it landed I picked it up, saying, 'I heard somewhere that it's lucky to keep it,' and I placed it superstitiously beside my place at the table, but added, 'but I don't really need luck, not when I've got friends like you.'

'And Greg,' Denise put in.

'And Greg,' I repeated, and felt a slight pang of regret that I hadn't invited him as Denise had suggested earlier in the week.

'To friends, then.' Adam had filled the glasses and now he handed us a glass each, raising his to clink it with ours. 'Whoops,' he suddenly turned to go, explaining over his shoulder, 'I think I can smell something burning.'

Denise rushed after him, and I could hear them laughing together in the kitchen as they put right whatever had gone wrong. I envied them the closeness of their relationship, but didn't grudge them their happiness for a moment, appreciating what they had both been through to reach this point in their lives, Denise going through the grief of losing a much-loved husband and Adam surviving an unhappy marriage and a bitter divorce. I just wondered if there was someone so right out there for me.

It would have been nice to think that there was, but for the moment I knew I had enough to do getting on with a life that seemed suddenly full of all kinds of possibilities.

# 10

I have no idea how long I stood there with a glass of champagne in one hand and the burned down taper — now extinguished — in the other, mesmerized by the thought of the future that awaited me, the life that was finally filled with promise.

The strident ringing of the doorbell brought me back to the present. In fact, it made me jump and I spilled a little of my drink before setting the glass carefully and a little guiltily on the tablecloth over the damp patch I had made.

I walked into the hall, calling, 'I'll get it, shall I?'

'Would you mind?' Denise called back, adding, 'No idea who it could be. We're not expecting anyone else, are we, Adam?'

I didn't hear his reply because I was already at the door, reaching for the latch and coming face to face with Max — the arrogant and very rude — Graham.

For a moment he seemed as stunned to see me as I was to see him and then, evidently remembering the manners he'd shown no sign of the last time we met, he thrust his hand forward and said, 'Max Graham. I don't believe I've had the pleasure.'

I couldn't believe it. He had no bloody idea who I was, and yet precious little time had passed since we last met, and in this very house.

'Max,' Denise came bustling out, a tea towel tied around her slim waist, 'we weren't expecting you, were we? Oh, and you remember Jo, don't you?'

It should have been comical, but I didn't find it so, watching Max struggle to recall just who the hell I was and where on earth we might have met before.

Had I really changed that much, and in so short a time? It appeared that I had indeed, because if ever I needed proof that *fine feathers maketh man* — or woman — it was standing there right in front of me. His floundering behaviour made me wonder if I'd been a complete gargoyle before and nobody had thought to tell me.

Stung, I said, quite sharply, 'Oh, I expect Max meets lots of women — and men,' I added, almost as an afterthought, 'in his line of work — and what *was* that again, Max? You can't expect him to remember them all.'

He rose to the challenge and said smoothly, 'Of course I remember you. I never forget a pretty face.'

I almost said out loud, 'Oh, pu-lease,' but then I remembered I was in someone else's house and that this was a friend of theirs and forced myself to smile as if I was accepting the compliment instead.

'Come on through,' Denise was saying, adding to my complete and utter horror, 'you must join us, there's plenty to go round. Adam has cooked enough food for an army.'

For a moment I thought she and Adam had set this up and I felt like killing the pair of them. However, Max's protestations seemed genuine enough even to someone like me who was hardly his biggest fan.

'Oh, no,' he seemed most embarrassed, and waving a sheaf of paperwork, said, 'I only dropped by with these. They could have waited until Monday, but I'll be in London then and Adam did say he was waiting for them.'

'The plans for the next lot of conversions,' Adam reached out to grasp them with an eagerness that didn't appear to be forced or false. 'Excellent. With work drying up all around us, and similar companies going under, it's great to have the next job already in hand. Jo will be pleased about that because her son is part of my workforce.'

'Must be a good lad then,' Max nodded,

smiling his charming smile. 'Adam only employs the best.'

He obviously knew how to say the right thing — some of the time — and in spite of myself I began to warm to him, but only a little bit, just enough to offer, 'I'll go and set another place, shall I?'

I went off to do just that, familiar enough with Denise's house to know where everything was kept, and was disconcerted when Max joined me in the dining room. I concentrated on the job in hand, leaving him to find something to say and feeling only satisfaction when he appeared to be struggling. I imagined he was a man who would rarely be lost for words.

In the end he said, quite quietly, 'Is it my imagination, or do we seem to have got off on the wrong foot?'

I smiled at him sweetly and said, 'I don't know, do we? You tell me.'

'Oh, dear,' he said humbly, 'I have no idea what I might have done to make you dislike me so intensely, but whatever it is, or was, I do apologize most profusely. Do you think it's at all possible for us to start all over again? Please?'

He looked like a puppy dog pleading for forgiveness for some misdemeanour. I almost expected him to sit up and beg, and my resolve weakened still further. After all, it was hardly Max's fault I'd gone to town on my appearance and how could I really blame him for not recognizing me when I scarcely recognized myself these days? However, that said, I wasn't going to be too encouraging.

'Why not?' I shrugged carelessly, and turned my attention to folding a napkin just so.

'Thank you.'

I hadn't realized Max had come to stand so close behind me and I almost crashed into him when I turned around. He thrust out a hand as if we had indeed just met and reluctantly I put mine into a grasp that was surprisingly firm and warm around my colder fingers.

'I'm Max Graham, long-time friend and business associate of Adam Mitchell and I hope Denise also now counts me as a friend. Perhaps in time you will too. It's Jo, isn't it?'

'I'm surprised you've remembered,' I said, sounding a little sour even to myself. I wasn't usually so slow to forgive and wasn't sure exactly what my problem was when the guy was obviously going out of his way to be pleasant. A case of too little too late, I supposed, and he *had* been *very* rude the first time we met, behaving as if I was beneath his notice.

I was ill-prepared when I was treated to the full one hundred watt smile Max turned on as he reminded me, 'Denise reintroduced you to me when I came in just now, remember, and even my short-term memory isn't that bad.' He laughed and I couldn't help but join in, especially when he asked, 'Friends, please?'

'Oh, go on then.' I shook his hand. 'I'm Josephine Farrell, a work colleague of Denise.'

He didn't let go of my hand, but looking right into my eyes he assured me, 'I promise I will never forget you again. I have no idea how it could have happened the first time around.'

The last thing I wanted to do at that moment was to remind him of the dowdy woman I had been. 'Don't give it another thought,' I urged, adding wryly, 'I probably won't remember *you* next time we meet. If there is a next time.'

'Oh,' he said very seriously, 'I intend to make very sure there *is* a next time.'

I couldn't believe it. Max Graham was *flirting* with me and I was suddenly elated and also filled with total confusion. It had been so long that I'd forgotten how that felt and how to reciprocate.

It was a relief when Denise came in with

hot dishes to set on the table, and laughing she told Max, 'Oh, put her down, do, you old philanderer you. Lead my friend Jo astray and you'll have me to deal with.'

'Well, that's nice, isn't it?' Max looked the very picture of innocence, and we were all laughing when Adam came in, querying, 'What's going on in here? I hope you haven't started the party without me.'

That set the tone for an evening that was friendly, funny and very flirty. I couldn't recall a time in recent years that I had enjoyed myself more. It felt as if we were two established couples, even though that was plainly ridiculous given that Max and I had only just really met for the first time. I'd decided by then not even to count that other time and refused to let it ruin whatever was going on between us — because something was. I might have been out of practice with relationships but even I realized that.

I wasn't surprised when Max offered to run me home in his car. Once he realized I didn't drive it would have appeared churlish of him not to, though that hadn't seemed to stop him last time. I had to push that thought away quite firmly and somehow I managed it.

I didn't know much about cars, obviously, being a non-driver, but the one I climbed into was a very attractive sleek model, a bit like the owner, really.

'What on earth do you have in all those bags?' Max asked belatedly as he got in beside me, having previously loaded said bags into the boot.

'I went shopping with Denise,' I smiled, 'which is nearly always fatal to the bank balance.'

'I'm sure it was money well spent.' He turned the ignition key, and the engine purred into life and the car moved forward smoothly.

I wondered fleetingly what it would be like to drive such a car. In fact, I wondered what it would be like to drive and whether or not I was looking forward to finding out. I quailed inwardly at the thought of making that phone call on Monday. Distracted for a moment, I didn't realize that Max was still speaking.

'Sorry,' I said, 'I wasn't really listening. What did you say?'

He laughed, shaking his head at me. 'You really know how to make a guy feel special, don't you? Or are you still punishing me for my former memory lapse?'

I turned and smiled. 'Nothing of the sort, I just have a few things on my mind.'

'Me too,' Max agreed, adding, 'and one of them is you. I was asking if I could see you again.'

'Oh, you're bound to,' I said carelessly, not

catching on very quickly, which was hardly surprising, given my lack of experience, 'I'm often round at Denise's. You can stop here.' I indicated that he should pull over, which he did. 'I live in those flats over there. The one at the top that's in darkness because obviously I'm not at home.'

'I meant,' Max said, 'that I would like to take you out sometime — if you think you can stand another evening of my company.'

'Oh.'

It shouldn't have come as such a shock. On reflection, the whole evening had been leading up to this point. I supposed I should have realized it, but somehow I hadn't.

'You do make a man work, don't you? Would it help if I said please?'

I scraped up my scattered wits and put them back together in some semblance of order, determined to keep my cool. 'It might.'

Then we were both laughing and I found I was enjoying myself hugely and had stopped feeling nervous.

'You might have heard me tell Adam that I'm in London next week, but would it be all right if I gave you a ring when I get back? Do you have a mobile?'

I shook my head, 'Not me. I'm an old-fashioned girl. I have a phone in my house, and that's it, but you are welcome to ring me on that.'

'I'll just pop you into my blackberry.' Max took out something even I recognized must be a very expensive gadget and I felt I should be honoured to be added to the data therein, even if it was the modern equivalent of the little black book in his case.

I still couldn't resist joking, 'Sounds painful.'

He got out of the car and came to open the door for me, before collecting all the bags from the boot and offering to carry them up to the flat. I think we both knew it would be too much too soon and he didn't try to insist when I said I could easily manage.

'Thank you for the lift, Max. It was really kind of you.'

'It was my pleasure entirely,' he stood smiling down at me and, shaking his head, he said, 'I can't believe I could have forgotten you once we'd met, Jo, but I can promise you it won't happen again.' Then he kissed me very gently on my cheek and stood on the kerb watching me. He was still standing there when I reached my own flat and, without switching a light on, went to the window and looked out.

I would have run down to Greg's flat to tell him all about it, but I'd noticed that his flat, too, had been in darkness and I wondered fleetingly where he had spent the evening and whether it was with someone nice. I hoped so, because he deserved to be happy, as happy as I was right at that moment.

★ ★ ★

'Well,' said Denise, the moment she walked into the office on Monday and before she had even removed her jacket, 'I don't know what you've done to Max but I've never seen him so smitten.'

'Oh, rubbish,' I scoffed, shaking my head at her, 'he's a born flirt and it doesn't mean a thing to him.'

'That's where you're wrong,' she insisted, taking off her coat and hanging it up, patting her hair and putting her handbag into a desk drawer. She then paused, obviously for dramatic effect, and said, 'He was on the phone to Adam *first thing* yesterday morning wanting to know all about you. We weren't even up, for God's sake. He said he's never met anyone like you before.'

'But he has met me before — and I made such a great impression last time he didn't even know who the hell I was when we met again.' I couldn't help that it still rankled sometimes.

'Can you really blame him, Jo? Now come on, be totally honest with me. I'm your friend, remember, and even I hardly recognize you.'

'Thanks. Is that supposed to make me feel better?'

'Yes, it's supposed to make you feel *great*. You wanted to make changes and the change in you is phenomenal — and you haven't even had surgery, just a haircut, a bit of make-up and some new outfits. Bloody hell, woman, you could even give Helen Mirren a run for her money these days.'

I burst into tears then, and Denise would never be able to work out, not in a million years, that there was nothing she could have said that would have made me happier. I realized I had a lot to thank Helen Mirren for and the award-winning actress would never even know.

'I'm being an idiot, aren't I?' I mopped my eyes and tried to smile.

'He really likes you, Jo,' Denise said seriously, 'and even if you don't want him, it must make you feel good to think that a man like Max, who can have his pick of women, is so eager to take you out.'

I realized then that I knew precious little about the man, so I spent the rest of the day coaxing every little detail out of Denise. The more I learned, the more I wondered what on earth I was getting into because it soon became painfully obvious that the man was way out of my league.

To someone who had never had much in the way of money, it sounded as if Max was literally rolling in the stuff, though Denise described him as merely 'comfortably off'. He was apparently a property developer and highly successful in his field, which I didn't doubt for a moment. He was obviously used to the high life, while I was only used to my life. Max exuded confidence while my own was newfound, exceptionally fragile, and couldn't be expected to cope with someone of his experience for what was destined to be the briefest alliance. What it really came down to, I decided, was that he was too good for the likes of me.

'Nonsense,' said Greg staunchly, when I finally caught him at home. 'Money and a certain lifestyle doesn't make him a better person. Any man would be proud to have you on his arm.'

'Would you?' I found myself asking without having any idea why.

'Damn sure.' To his credit he didn't hesitate for a moment.

'Well, he probably won't ring,' I said, not quite sure whether to feel relieved or disappointed at the thought.

'He will,' Greg sounded pretty confident, but added, 'Meanwhile don't just sit around waiting until he does. How about those cake decorating classes? Do you still want to go? And did you book the driving lessons yet?'

'Yes. No. And no I haven't booked myself in with a clairvoyant either, as it happens. What have you ticked off *your* list, which is, of course, *much* shorter than mine?'

'I've picked up holiday brochures,' he snatched them up from the coffee table and waved them triumphantly under my nose, 'and I think I've fallen in love with the travel agent — although,' he added doubtfully, 'I think she might be a bit young for me *and* she was wearing a wedding ring.'

'Well, that won't do. Where were you thinking of going?' I asked nosily, contrarily feeling a little put out that he was getting on with his list without my help, which was just plain stupid. He wouldn't want me holding his hand any more than I would want him holding mine.

'Perhaps the Maldives,' he said thoughtfully. 'That's one place I've never been, but I've been told it's absolutely beautiful. Why don't you come?'

'Me?' I sat up straight. 'Why?'

'Why not? We're friends, aren't we, and

holidaying abroad is on your list, isn't it? It might be fun.'

'Mmm, I'll have to think about that one,' I felt sick at the thought of getting on a plane, but I didn't tell him that, just encouraged, 'Don't wait for me, though. I'll have enough to be getting on with, what with the cake decorating we're going to do and the driving lessons to book.'

'Here you are then, no time like the present.' Greg handed me the phone.

I stared at it as if it was a stick of dynamite, but made no move to take the instrument from him. 'What am I meant to do with that?'

'Book those driving lessons. What else? Don't tell me you don't have the little business card Denise gave you in your bag because I know you do.'

'Oh, but I — '

Taking my hand, Greg placed the phone right in it and encouraged, 'Just do it. I promise you'll feel so much better when you have.'

He was right, of course, but then Greg usually was, I'd found. After speaking to the instructor I felt so much more confident. He had pupils much older than I was, he assured me. He wasn't expecting me to know the first thing about driving a car, and he actually preferred it that way, as a matter of fact.

When Greg booked us in for the cake decorating classes immediately after that I think we were both elated. We sat grinning at each other and let our tea go cold.

'I reckon we should make a start on that sitting room of yours next,' he rubbed his hands eagerly, 'before we both get so booked up that we have no time to spare.'

'Oh, Greg,' I pulled a face, 'I'm not sure I can live with yet more mess and upheaval, I've only just got the bedroom straight.'

'But you want it done, don't you? It would be a shame to stop now, wouldn't it? Shall I put the kettle on again while you have a think about it?'

'No, thanks, no more tea, but I'll sleep on it. I know you're right and it would be nice to see it done, but — '

Greg was seeing me out when he suddenly said, 'I think I have the answer.'

I stopped, smiled and said, 'Have I missed something? What was the question?'

'Why don't you move in here and I move into yours until the decorating is done? If I get a shift on I could give the kitchen and bathroom a coat of emulsion, too, and then it would, literally, be *all* done. What do you think?'

My mouth flapped. There was no other word for the way it opened and closed with no sound coming out.

Eventually I found my voice. 'You can't possibly do that,' I protested.

'Because?'

'I couldn't ask it of you.'

'You haven't,' Greg pointed out mildly, 'I've offered.'

'But your time.'

'Is my own. You can say it's clearing number six on my list.'

I came to a sudden decision, 'All right then,' I said recklessly, 'but only if I can do something for you in return.'

'Oh, you can.' He laughed then, and looked so ridiculously pleased that I had a moment to regret my rash offer and to wonder what on earth he was going to ask from me. 'You can come to the Maldives and tick number six off *your* list. I'll make a start on your living room tomorrow.'

# 11

I walked up the stairs in a daze, wondering how on earth I'd become committed to allowing Greg to complete the renovation of my flat in what sounded like was going to be only a matter of days, and to going on a foreign holiday with him to boot.

The former was bad enough because it meant I was taking still further advantage of Greg's generous nature. The latter was actually unthinkable for someone who was bordering on phobic about flying, yet I had no idea how I was going to get out of it, especially as I was the one who had struck the bloody bargain in the first place.

Bumping into Edna on the landing was all I needed. She had her coat on, but it was difficult to tell if she was just going into her flat or just coming out. Indeed, I even wondered if it was just another way she'd devised of justifying her presence on the landing outside of our front doors, since there was only so much polishing you could do even if you were as totally obsessed with cleanliness as Edna appeared to be.

'Oh, Mrs Farrell. Josephine. I'm glad I've caught you.'

'Why what's the matter, Miss Gutheridge?' I asked, trying to hide my impatience and reminding myself yet again that she was just lonely and probably *not* just the nosy old busybody she gave such a good impression of being.

'There was a gentleman here earlier on looking for you. He was knocking at your door for quite some time. I only noticed because I just happened to be polishing my letterbox when he first arrived and then when I came out to sweep the landing he was still there.'

'He could have come to the wrong flat,' I pointed out. 'How do you know he was looking for me?' I already knew what the answer was going to be and, as soon as I heard it, any goodwill I had managed to force myself to feel towards Edna dissolved as quickly as it came. She *was* a nosy old busybody, nothing more and nothing less.

'Well, I asked if I could help, of course. It would have been churlish of me not to. He asked for you by name. Mrs Josephine Farrell, he said, so I confirmed that you lived there and then he wondered what time you might be back, and I said you were usually home from work by that time, but must have stopped off somewhere.' She gave a telling glance towards the stairs and I wondered why she hadn't made it her business to tell this unknown caller exactly where I was and who with. I was frankly impressed by this unusual sign of reticence on her part, but it didn't make me feel any more kindly towards her.

'Very kind of you, I'm sure,' I said sourly, somehow refraining from reminding her that she could have just ignored the guy, leaving him to come back and try another time. Which was what he would have to do anyway. I was about to turn away, but then thought to ask, 'What did he look like?'

Edna brightened at this show of interest on my part, and asked eagerly, 'Do you think you might know him, then?'

'I've really no idea, Miss Gutheridge, because I don't know what he looks like, do I?'

My tone was dripping with sarcasm, but Edna appeared not even to notice, as she laughed a surprisingly merry laugh and said, 'Silly me, of course you don't. Well,' she puffed right up with the importance of the information she was about to impart, 'he was tall, very tall, and distinguished looking. Short grey hair, smart clothes, pleasant face and very charming manner.'

She waited with bated breath for me to

identify my visitor, but I kept my expression carefully blank and told her, 'No idea who that might be. Someone from work needing some information perhaps or someone collecting for charity. Whoever it is will call back if it's important,' I said over my shoulder as I pushed my key in the lock and turned it, 'but thank you. I really appreciate your attention to my affairs, though I'm sure you have far more important things you could be dealing with.'

I closed the door firmly in her face and leaned back against it. Honestly, you couldn't move for the woman but on this occasion at least, it appeared she had her uses. I could feel my lips turning up into a delighted smile. There was little doubt about it. From Edna's description, Max was already back and keen to get in touch. I felt a little flutter of excitement that was totally unfamiliar to me and I didn't even try to deny that I was looking forward to seeing him again.

As if the upsurge in my previously non-existent love life wasn't enough, the very next morning Greg was on my step bright and early with a small suitcase at his feet.

'Well, I know I only live downstairs,' he said, breezing in, 'but it's best not to have to keep running back for essentials.'

'You're moving in *today*?' I stood in the

open doorway and stared along the hallway after him. 'But we only talked about it last night, Greg. It might not be the best time.'

'When would be then?' he was already in the kitchen, filling the kettle by the sound of it.

The clatter of Edna's letterbox reminded me of her neverending surveillance, and I paused to wonder if she ever slept, before I went inside and firmly closed the front door behind me. That was all I needed, for Edna to think we were living together in some sort of permanent arrangement.

'Well, there's so much else going on.' I could hear myself making excuses, when we both knew I wanted nothing more than for the refurbishment of my flat to be done and dusted. 'I've got the driving lessons booked, we've got the cake decorating classes to go to, and how am I going to find the time to go and choose the paint. I have to go to work.'

'Look,' Greg came to stand in front of me and he took my two hands into his, 'this is perfectly straightforward, a coat of emulsion or two on the walls and white paintwork. I know you hate magnolia and love the clotted cream colour in the hall, so you can leave it to me to get the paint and pay me back later. Pushing the furniture to the centre of the room is all it will take. You've been decluttering for weeks so there aren't too many knick-knacks around any more.

'While I'm picking up the paint for that, I can collect a paint chart and if you fancy anything different for the bathroom or kitchen, just tell me. The decorating can be finished before this week is out, Jo, and if you fancy changing carpets, curtains or furniture you can do it as the mood takes you.'

'But you're giving up *all* of your time,' I wailed, quite determined to look and feel guilty, though I had to work to keep the eager note out of my voice.

'It's one week,' he pointed out persuasively, still holding my hands, 'and a small price for me to pay for the way knowing you has changed my life. Don't you see, when you invited me in to your home and I watched you make that list and step out of your rut, comfort zone, whatever you want to call it, you inspired me to do the same. Whatever I do for you now can never repay *you* for giving me my life back.'

'Oh, Greg, you don't have to repay me. That's what friends are for.'

'But that's the whole point, I didn't have any friends, Jo. I turned my back on them along with my old life when Monica died. I've been little more than a recluse these past years, and then I came up to borrow the

*Advertiser* and everything changed.'

We ended up hugging and it didn't feel strange or awkward, because we were friends, after all.

'Oh, my God, will you look at the time.' A glance at my watch sent me into a panic. 'I've got to go. I don't have time to pack a case now, so I'll do it when I get home — if you're sure you don't mind me moving into your place, just for the duration. I've honestly had my fill of upheaval and of the smell of paint. You can come down for your meals if you can put up with my cooking, and I don't have to tell you to help yourself to anything you need while you're living in my space.'

'Ditto,' Greg said. 'Now scoot, because you're going to be late.'

The rest of the week passed in a blur and I barely had time even to notice I was sleeping in the wrong bed because I was out like a light as soon as my head touched Greg's pillow each night.

My first driving lesson appeared to me to go exceptionally badly, though Derek, the instructor, was pleasant, chatty and did his best to put me at my ease. He also chose a long, straight, and fairly unfrequented road for my introduction to seat positions, mirrors, handbrake, gears, indicators and all the million and one important items and checks I was never going to remember. Every single instruction went into one ear and out of the other without as much as a second's pause and at a speed that made my head spin.

I started shaking the moment I got behind the wheel and didn't stop until Greg met me at the door of his own flat, took one look at my anguished expression, poured me a stiff brandy and listened as I told him, in no uncertain terms, that I was never going to get behind the wheel of a car again.

When I had finished ranting he put a plate of chilli con carne in front of me and told me, 'You can do it, Jo,' so firmly that I had no choice but to believe him and agree not to cancel the lesson I had booked for the following week.

The first cake decorating class was much more fun, with the lesson involving covering the Victoria sandwiches we had been instructed to bring along with rolled out fondant icing. The tutor demonstrated adeptly, making the whole exercise appear deceptively simple. The end result had a top as flat as an ice rink, the covering dropped smoothly down the sides to meet the board where any excess was cut neatly away with a sharp knife.

It quickly became apparent that thinly rolled icing handled by an expert behaved in a completely different way in amateur hands. There was a great deal of laughter as sheets of sugar paste fell this way and that, but seldom squarely onto the prepared cake, and rarely in one piece. There was more and pretty embarrassed laughter when it was noted that the best results had been achieved by the only man in the class of twelve people — Greg himself.

'I think you showed up one or two self-professed 'experts' there,' I told him as we clattered up the stairs, pausing on Greg's landing to bid each other goodnight.

'Beginner's luck,' he said modestly. 'They have nothing to fear from me.' He indicated the two cake boxes. 'What are we going to do with these? We'll never eat them both.'

'I'll take mine into work. Denise has her family coming to stay for the weekend, so it will soon disappear. Actually,' I made a face, 'can I give her yours because mine looks a bit of a mess? And if I'm being totally honest your sponge puts mine in the shade, too.'

Greg laughed, 'Go on then.' He put his box on top of mine, 'Can you manage if I open the door for you? An early night wouldn't go amiss for me.'

'Yes, that'll be great. I'll be happy to go straight to bed, too, although I was going to ask if I could come up and take a quick peek

162

at what you've done so far.'

Free of his cake box, Greg was able to wag a finger under my nose and chide, 'Now then, don't be so impatient. You can see it when it's done, and then I expect you to praise me to the skies and tell me what a marvellous job I've done.'

I laughed and was still laughing as I carried the cakes into the peace and comfort of my downstairs neighbour's flat and went to unload the boxes and put the kettle on. I was on my way to bed carrying a cup of herb tea and the latest celebrity magazine when the phone rang, breaking the silence. I was shocked and only then realized it was the first time I had heard the phone ring in Greg's flat in all the time I'd known him.

I hesitated, but then realized I'd better answer it in case it was something important. I could always take a message.

'Fancy not telling your only child that you've moved house,' Petie's voice admonished before I could say a word. 'I wondered what the heck was going on when a man answered your phone and said you were living somewhere else. I can't keep up with you these days, Mother.'

I was torn between laughing and crying, and instantly filled with horrendous guilt because, with so much going on in my own life, I'd all but forgotten what was happening in Petie's.

Well, no, that wasn't strictly true — of course I hadn't really forgotten, just persuaded myself to put it all to the back of my mind and put my faith in Petie doing the right thing about the situation he was in, whatever the right thing was.

I decided not to launch into explanations, feeling sure that Greg would already have filled Petie in, as turned out to be the case as the conversation continued.

'Well, you've found me now, and it's lovely to hear from you.'

'I've tried a couple of times to catch you in,' he didn't sound cross, quite the contrary, in fact, 'but you're a hard woman to pin down these days. Why you haven't got a mobile or even an answerphone, I'll never know.'

'Never had any use for either,' I was dismissive, but the thought that Petie might not be the only one trying to get hold of me suddenly made the idea of owning either quite appealing. I realized I'd all but forgotten about Max looking for me, too, with the current busyness of my life and that did surprise me. I wondered with a little smirk how many times *he* had tried to ring me before calling round.

'Any idea when you'll be back in your own

flat?' Petie queried, 'only I was going to bring Lizzie round to meet you.'

Lizzie. Petie's *significant other* who had become so, in my eyes at least, because she was the mother of my unborn grandchild. I quailed at the thought of so important a meeting, because what if I hated her? More importantly, what if she hated me? Our relationship could affect my relationship with my son and with his child for many years to come if they decided their future was going to be together.

'Did Greg give any indication when you were speaking to him?' I queried.

'He seemed to think it would all be finished by the weekend. Really nice guy, isn't he? You seem to have him twisted round your little finger,' Petie laughed as he added, 'I can't believe you've been so damn cheeky, not only getting him decorating your pad, but persuading him to live with the mess and the smell of paint while you make yourself at home in his probably very nice flat.'

I laughed, too, but made it clear, 'Greg did make the offer — both of them — and it was one I couldn't refuse and justify the refusal. I know it sounds cheeky, but we are good friends. He's been quite lonely since his wife died, with too much time on his hands.'

'He was telling me. Probably thought I was

entitled to an explanation, but you are a grown woman, so there was really no need. I trust you not to do anything silly. I think I've done enough stupid things in my life for both of us, but that, my dear mother, is about to change.'

He would say no more, and left it to me to ring him when I was back home and ready for visitors, and by the end of that week I was. Greg was in his own flat with a pot of tea waiting when I got in from work on Friday, showered, dressed casually but neatly, and looking extremely pleased with himself.

'It's all done,' he said, helping me off with my coat, 'and I've put the furniture back where it was. If you fancy a change I can move it again, of course. I've had the windows wide open all day, so the smell of paint isn't too strong as far as I can tell, but someone told me today that an onion cut in half will do the trick.'

I sipped my tea, and said, 'You've been out then, that's good, because Edna will swear I've been holding you prisoner up there and forcing you to decorate twenty-four hours a day.'

'No,' Greg laughed at the idea, 'I haven't been out, but some guy came to the door looking for you and he told me about the onion.'

Max hadn't given up yet then, I felt ridiculously pleased. 'Did he give his name?' I asked curiously, and when Greg shook his head I added, in what I hoped was an off-hand way, 'What did he look like?' I took a casual sip of tea as if the answer couldn't have mattered less.

'Tall, taller than me, grey hair and grey beard and not unlike Sean Connery to look at. Why, do you think you might know him?'

The tea went down the wrong way, which necessitated a lot of coughing on my part and a good deal of back thumping on Greg's. I was grateful for the diversion, because his answer wasn't what I had been expecting at all.

The man on my doorstep wasn't Max at all, definitely not. It had taken the Sean Connery comparison for me to put an identity to the mystery caller, who had now called and missed me twice, and obviously wasn't about to give up. Now, I realized with a feeling of absolute horror, that my past had come back to haunt me, and show my life up for the tissue of lies it was.

If Jack Farrell really was looking for me, and there seemed little doubt that he was, then the days of playing the respectable widow were well and truly over.

# 12

After a sleepless night, during which I relived most of a marriage in which the bad times were pretty horrendous and far outweighed any good times, I was up before daylight and desperate to talk to someone.

The problem was, of course, that no one knew Jack Farrell was still living and breathing because when I told people I had 'lost' him, I had never gone on to add it was to another woman and that she was only the last in a long list.

I was at a complete loss but then brightened considerably when I realized that, in fact, *one* person did know the truth — apart from Petie. Even he didn't know the whole story but still wanted as little to do with his father as I did and would definitely not appreciate hearing that he was back in the area and trying to get in touch. That person was Denise. Unfortunately for my state of mind, Denise was not an early riser at the weekends so five o'clock on a Saturday morning would definitely not be a good time to be ringing her.

I spent the next few hours frantically

polishing and tidying the home that Jack and I had once shared — anything to keep myself occupied — appreciating as I did so just how much the flat had changed with Greg's help, finally resembling the sort of home I had always wanted.

For years I had given the real circumstances of Jack's departure little thought, and if I had, having been so long without him I could almost believe my husband really was dead. However, the reality was he was very much alive and I felt really bad now to think I had allowed a friendship that meant so much to me to be based on this massive lie. Not only that, but that I had allowed Greg to go on believing that we shared the experience of losing a partner when I could easily have set the record straight on countless occasions.

Windows were cleaned with far more energy than I normally gave to such a detested task, every kitchen surface was scoured, and every other surface was polished to within an inch of its life. Wardrobes and drawers were ruthlessly cleared of garments that didn't meet my exacting present requirements, along with anything around the place that could be termed 'clutter'.

When I'd finished, every room was gleaming, there were more bulging black bags ready to be handed in to the charity shop, I'd showered and dressed, and it wasn't even nine o'clock. However, I was desperate by then and could wait no longer to make the call. To my relief the phone was picked up pretty swiftly and I was heartened by Denise's alert tone. Even so, I began by apologizing.

'Sorry, Denise, I'm so sorry to be ringing so early on a weekend. I know how you love your lie-in and I wouldn't disturb you if it wasn't an emergency.'

She pounced onto the word. 'Emergency? What sort of emergency?'

I shook my head, even though she couldn't see the gesture, 'No, that's the wrong word, but I couldn't think of a better one. I didn't wake you, did I?'

'No,' Denise soothed, 'I was up and playing the doting granny, so that Bobbi and Jason could sleep in.'

'I'm taking you away from your grand-daughter.'

'No, you're not, Jo, because Adam has just taken her off to the newsagent with him. Now come on, tell all. Something's on your mind for you to be ringing this early on a Saturday morning.'

There was no other way to say it than just to spit it out without dressing the facts up or down. 'Jack's back.'

'Jack who?' Denise began, then gave a great

gasp as the penny dropped with a deafening clang and, as if she still couldn't believe it, she queried in a horrified whisper, 'Not *your* Jack?'

'He's not *mine*,' I denied furiously, 'I don't want him.'

'No, I know,' she added hastily, 'I just couldn't think of any other way of describing him.'

'I can think of a few ways of describing him,' I told her bitterly, 'and none of them is polite or flattering.'

'Have you seen him, then?'

'No, but he's called round at the flat twice now when I wasn't home, because first Edna and then Greg saw him. He didn't give his name either time, but the description fits. It's him all right.'

'Bloody hell.'

'My sentiments exactly,' I retorted and then wailed, 'What on earth am I going to do, Denise? Everyone but you thinks I'm widowed, I can't suddenly have a dead husband popping up. I'll be a laughing stock.'

'Now calm down,' Denise advised, 'and let's think this through properly. If I know you — and I think I do after all these years — you wouldn't have come right out and said you were widowed, you're far too honest.'

'No,' I said dubiously, 'but would I have

talked about 'losing' my husband?'

'Well, you did, but you lost him to another woman and not the grim reaper. Anyway, to be blunt, it's no one's business but your own. I don't even know why you told me the truth, and if you hadn't and I found out it wouldn't matter a jot to me. Being friends doesn't mean we're entitled to a full CV. I'm sure we all have secrets and I certainly had mine but, as Adam has so rightly said, we all have a past and are entitled to keep it there.'

I knew Denise was referring to the death of her baby boy many years before when she was still a teenager, but it was hardly the same. Had he lived, been adopted and been liable to come knocking at her door, I might have seen some similarities.

I didn't say any of this but instead pointed out, 'I had to tell you, didn't I? My marital status is there in my record at work.'

'The only thing I've ever checked in your record is the length of your service with Cheapsmart, so that you get your additional holiday entitlement. Jo, I don't even know your real age. Anyway, this isn't getting us anywhere, but the point I was trying to make — rather clumsily, perhaps — is that if it's telling Greg you're worried about, I think you will find he feels exactly as I do, that basically it is none of our damn business. If it bothers you, just go right down now and tell him the truth.'

Denise made it sound so simple, and I knew she was probably right, but it didn't deal with my real concern.

'But what does Jack want, suddenly turning up out of the blue like that?' I worried. 'I haven't seen him since — '

'Since he cleared off with his floozy, taking everything with him that wasn't nailed down — including Petie's piggy bank I seem to remember you telling me — and the little bit of money you had put away to pay the bills.'

I laughed without humour. 'You don't forget much, do you?'

'I was just trying to remind you, in case you needed reminding, that whatever he's come back for will be for his own benefit, for sure, and not for yours. A leopard never changes his spots, Jo, especially this particular leopard. Just remember that you don't owe him a damn thing.'

'I know you're right,' I agreed, 'but I just wish I had an inkling about his intentions.'

'Are you afraid of him?' Denise suddenly sounded worried, 'because if so — '

'I'm not,' I said firmly, wondering even as I said it whether it was strictly true. 'I'm not,' I repeated, adding, 'not any more.'

'If he turns up, phone me, or Greg. You

don't have to talk to him on your own and, remember, you don't owe him a thing.'

The doorbell rang then, and I physically jumped, almost dropping the phone in my panic and then froze. It was only Denise's voice calling me that made me move and I whispered into the mouthpiece, 'What if that's him?'

'Open the door,' she ordered, 'and if it is him, say his name very loudly so that I can hear. I can be there in less than ten minutes and I'll get Jason out of bed and bring him with me.'

My heart was thumping so loudly it sounded like a drumbeat in my ears as I made my way to the door on legs that felt like overcooked spaghetti. I could see a tall shadow through the frosted glass and my hand visibly shook as I reached to turn the latch. For the first time ever, I prayed that Edna would be on the landing polishing her letterbox.

The biggest bouquet of flowers I had ever seen in my life filled the doorway, concealing the identity of the caller and, in spite of myself, I laughed out loud. Someone had obviously been given the wrong address.

'I'm sorry, but you appear to have had a wasted journey up two flights of stairs, because those clearly aren't for me.'

'Wrong on both counts.' The deep voice filtering through the blooms brought me out in goosebumps even before the flowers were lowered to reveal a smiling Max Graham.

'Oh,' I said feebly, standing there like an idiot, as a variety of very different emotions raced through my mind.

'So,' Max was laughing down at me, looking a little bemused at my reaction to both his visit and his flowers, 'are you going to invite me in, or would you prefer to go out?'

'Go out?' I said stupidly, 'I'm not dressed for going out.'

'You look great to me.' Max sounded as if he meant it and more goosebumps erupted at the appreciative way he looked me up and down.

I'd never been so relieved for the massive wardrobe clearance that had seen every tatty and baggy garment confined to bin bags. The jeans and T-shirt I wore might have been casual but they were modern and, best of all they fitted the much slimmer figure I had recently acquired. I felt good and even I knew I looked it — for my age.

'You'd better come in.'

I took the flowers, inhaling the heady scent of the roses I could see peeping from among spectacular peonies in palest pink and mop-headed cream hydrangeas as I turned and led the way, picking up the phone as I passed it to reassure Denise, 'Everything is fine. I'll speak to you later.'

'Is that Max's voice I can hear?' Denise demanded, adding, 'It is, isn't it?'

'Mmm,' I murmured noncommittally, and repeating, 'I'll talk to you later,' I put the phone gently back onto its stand.

'I'll just put these in water,' I said, leading the way into a kitchen that was gleaming, thanks to my early ministrations and Greg's decorating skills. 'Though I wonder if I have a vase that's big enough. They are very beautiful, thank you. Can I get you a tea or a coffee?'

Before I could do either, or he could reply, the telephone rang.

'Do you mind if I get that?'

Max shook his head, still smiling and offered, 'I'll put the kettle on, shall I?'

He was slipping off his black leather jacket as I left the room, and I could already hear the sound of the tap running as I picked up the receiver.

'You're back in then,' came Petie's eager voice. 'How's it looking?'

'It's lovely,' I said truthfully. 'Greg has done a great job. I really owe him.'

'He sounded as if he was only too pleased

to help. So — when can we come round then? Is now a good time?'

'Erm, actually I have company.'

'Oh,' Petie sounded shocked, as well he might, since I'd gone from the being sort of mum who had very few friends, went nowhere and was always available, to someone who was the complete opposite. He recovered quickly and said, 'Say no more, except when would be a good time for you.'

I almost said I would get rid of my visitor, my instinct to be always there for my boy was very hard to ignore, but somehow I managed it and offered instead, 'Bring Lizzie round for supper, why don't you? About seven, then we'll have the whole evening to talk.'

I was taken aback when I walked back into the kitchen to find cups and saucers set out on a tray to which Max was adding a freshly made pot of tea. He'd even put the flowers in water, even if he had used the plastic bucket he must have found under the sink.

'You've been busy,' I said, pointing out reprovingly, 'but the bucket doesn't do the flowers justice and you've forgotten biscuits.'

'Ah,' he smacked a tanned hand to his forehead, 'I knew there was something missing.'

I found a packet of chocolate digestives and arranging them on a small plate, added them to the tray and asked, 'Kitchen or living-room.'

'Living room,' Max said promptly, 'just because I'm nosy and will enjoy seeing where you live.'

'Well,' I gathered up the tray and led the way, 'it's small, but it's cosy and it's home. That was my son on the phone. He's coming over with his girlfriend for supper later.'

'So, do we have the day then? Only I was rather hoping I could take you out to lunch.'

'That would be nice.' I didn't hesitate because I actually thought that it would be rather more than nice.

He sat with me on the couch and, though there was a whole vacant seat between us, I was very aware of his presence. Max wasn't someone you would easily be able to ignore, as I'd already found.

'Is he your only child?'

I smiled, 'Yes, and there are times when I've thought he was more than enough. A bit of a tearaway in his time — as Peter would readily admit — but he has turned his life around. Partly thanks to Adam, of course, who offered him a job when many might have thought twice.'

'Ah yes, I think I might have met him. If he's who I think he is, he's a nice lad.'

I glowed at the praise, and tried not to

think about Petie's latest crisis or what the outcome might be. 'Do you have any children?'

'Not to my knowledge and not from my marriage — I'm divorced,' he added, and I took the opportunity to add, 'Me, too,' pleased to have the chance to set the record straight early on, and determined I would do the same with Greg the minute I could.

'So — lunch then?' Max stood up and collecting the tray of tea things he went to set them down in the kitchen and pick his jacket up from where he'd left it on the back of a chair.

I hovered in the doorway. 'I should get changed.'

'Just put a jacket on — and perhaps some shoes.' He nodded at my fluffy slippers. 'You're fine as you are, honestly. Look, I'm wearing jeans, and anyway, if you change everything I get to spend even less time with you. I feel I need to rush you away before the phone goes again or someone else comes to the door.'

I relented, slipping on a new brown suede jacket and matching boots, since from the window I could see the day was overcast, deciding as I did so that I loved everything about my new wardrobe, especially the fact that I'd had Denise's far more expert guidance while making most of my purchases.

I didn't even care that Edna was positioned on the landing and busy with a spotless yellow duster, just bidding her a cheerful, 'Good morning,' as we went down the stairs.

There was no sign of Greg and I wasn't sure whether to be relieved or sorry. I was sure he'd be pleased for me; after all, why wouldn't he? Perhaps he was even out on a date of his own with the lady from the icing class who'd been paying him so much attention. It seemed strange, after so long spending every spare moment together that we were each suddenly off doing our own thing, but then I supposed that had been the whole object of the exercise, to get us out there and living our lives again.

Max held the passenger door of his gleaming car open for me and, as I climbed in, from the corner of my eye I saw a yellow duster flutter in the landing window and hoped Edna could find it in her to be glad for me.

Then, as Max turned the car round in the visitors' car park and began to make his way to the main road, all rational thought left me, for coming in the opposite direction was a dark-green Range Rover and at the wheel was no other than my ex-husband.

I looked right at Jack as the vehicles passed

and he looked right back at me. The difference was that, although I would have known him anywhere despite the fact he was greyer and older in appearance, he plainly had no idea who I was. I found that as liberating as hell and finally knew that all the effort I had put into reinventing myself was more than worth it.

# 13

I must have been smiling to myself because Max glanced my way and said, 'You look happy.'

'I've no reason not to be happy,' I told him, and suddenly knew it to be no more than the truth. Whatever Jack wanted or didn't want was immaterial because he no longer had the power to hurt me. I laughed at the sheer freedom of it all, and added, 'After all, the sun is shining and I'm being taken out to lunch by the man who just brought me flowers.'

'The very nice man who brought you flowers,' Max prompted cheekily, and waited.

I laughed again. 'The very, very nice man who brought me flowers — and the flowers were very, very nice, too. Thank you.'

'Do you like seafood?' he asked suddenly. 'Only I know this restaurant right across from the beach and the food there is the best I've ever tasted.'

'And you are, of course, a man of impeccable taste.'

'Exactly.'

The look he gave me somehow conveyed

that I was certainly to his taste and I shivered deliciously and pulled my jacket closer.

Max was obviously a regular and valued customer, and though the restaurant was busy, a table was quickly found for us with a view of the sea. Other diners greeted Max by name, looking at me curiously, but though polite he was brief in his dealings with them, making it clear his time was mine.

I hadn't been on a date since I was a teenager, and now I felt like that teenager all over again, young, carefree and with my life stretched out in front of me to do with as I pleased and to share with whom I pleased. I felt a great whoosh of sheer joy and hid my face behind the huge menu in case Max became concerned about sharing lunch with a grinning idiot.

'You can order it all if you like,' he sounded amused.

I looked at him over the top, and making a good effort at controlling my exuberance said, 'I'm spoiled for choice, and since I've always been indecisive, why don't I just leave it all to you? We've already decided you have impeccable taste.'

'A woman who trusts my judgement — an absolute paragon of wisdom — where has Denise been hiding you? And more importantly, *why* has she been hiding you?'

Now was the time to remind him that we had actually been introduced before — and when — but I suddenly realized I had no intention of explaining that I was that middle-aged mouse of a woman he'd determined at the time was beneath his notice. After all, why embarrass us both, I reasoned.

We settled down to eat and I was amazed to find that I was really enjoying myself, yet normally spending time with a man like Max, so confident and assured, would have frightened the life out of me. After so long without a man in my life it was hardly surprising I would feel much more at ease with someone like Greg, who had fears and insecurities that matched my own.

The difference was that though Greg was a very dear friend, with Max it felt as if there was the possibility of so much more. I hadn't been so attracted to a man since . . . I refused to even acknowledge his name and banished him resolutely from my mind. I would deal with his reappearance in my own good time.

When we left the restaurant, a stiff breeze had me buttoning my jacket, and Max turned me to him and pulled the collar up around my neck. He was so close I could feel his breath on my face and for a moment I thought he was going to kiss me.

'I was going to suggest a walk,' he said instead, 'but it's turned a bit chilly so perhaps we'd better give that a miss.'

'It's fine. I'm not really cold; it was just a bit of a shock stepping outside after the warmth in there. I could do with walking off the meal, especially as I'm expecting to be cooking supper later.' I laughed as I added, 'Not my favourite pastime, cooking, I should add, and I'm not even very good at it any more.' It seemed important to me that I didn't sell a false image of who I was and what I did.

Max laughed, too. He placed a casual arm around my shoulders, and gave me a quick hug before we started walking, saying, 'Well, that's what restaurants are for, isn't it? Someone has to keep them in business and I hope we can share many more meals in the future.'

'Oh, goodness,' I was suddenly horrified, 'I hope you don't think I was *hinting*, I was just trying to be truthful.'

He laughed even harder and, pulling me close, kissed the tip of my nose. 'Darling, it will be my pleasure, I assure you, but while you're being truthful, tell me what else you enjoy besides eating out. Theatre? Cinema?'

'Oh, everything is a novelty,' I said without thinking, 'it's been so long since I had a social life. I guess I allowed the divorce to knock my confidence and, anyway, I had a son to bring up. It's only quite recently I've really started to enjoy life again, and I don't mean that to sound self-pitying.'

'I find you refreshingly honest, Jo, a real breath of fresh air. Now I feel I must be honest with you, too. Since my divorce I know I've let my freedom go to my head, as Denise will probably tell you. She's so disapproved of my life and the kind of people I've shared it with. I'm not exactly poor and when you have money you're never short of company. After a failed marriage, I guess it did my bruised ego good to run around town with girls half my age on my arm. I'm only just beginning to see what I've been missing.'

By this time we were walking along the front with its souvenir shops and the arcades full of slot machines. We fed pots full of pennies into machines that ate the cash at an alarming rate with precious little to see in return. Max then spent a fortune trying to win a teddy bear for me, getting more and more frustrated when the grabber dropped the prize every time. He was inordinately pleased when he finally managed to lift the toy and cheered as it fell out of the chute and into my waiting hands.

'It's gorgeous but you could have bought it

in a shop for a fraction of what you've just spent,' I pointed out, hugging the brown bear, before pointing to the red heart it was holding with 'I love you', written across it in gold, 'and isn't that a bit premature?'

What could have been an extremely embarrassing moment ended up being one we both found hysterically funny, and I was proud of the way I had turned it around. The old me would have died on the spot or been rendered speechless and blushing from head to toe.

'We should eat candyfloss,' Max decided, pointing to where children were queuing. 'You can't visit the seaside without eating candyfloss.'

I tucked the bear into my pocket, leaving just his little face poking out, and said, 'Go ahead. I couldn't eat another thing. Oh,' I came suddenly to an abrupt standstill, 'look, a fortuneteller.'

'You don't believe all that stuff, do you?' he scoffed.

'But visiting one is on my list of things to do,' I said without thinking.

Before I had to explain, Max laughed and teased, 'Don't tell me — the list of one hundred things to do before you die. I thought those lists were supposed to have stuff like sky diving and bungee jumping on them.'

'Well, mine has visiting a clairvoyant on it, so would you mind terribly waiting while I have a reading? I have a feeling that if I don't do it now, I never will. You could go and get your candyfloss. I don't expect I will be in there very long; there's no queue.'

'Go on, then,' he smiled indulgently, obviously prepared to humour me, while clearly thinking it an odd thing for anyone to want to do. He took out his wallet, but I told him, 'I don't expect you to pay. I have my own money.'

I walked into what appeared to be little more than a hut. Inside, the walls of the small room were swathed in satin of various rich hues, and there was a chair set either side of a round table covered with a plush red chenille cloth, in the centre of which was a crystal ball. I wasn't sure whether to be excited or scared to death, especially when a young man came in, and not the Mystic Meg-type I was expecting.

I sat in the chair he indicated and he took the one opposite, saying, 'Place your hands on the table.'

He put his hands over my own and for a moment we sat in silence. My initial nerves just faded away and I waited eagerly to hear what he would say, but still managed to spend the time taking in his appearance. Possibly in his thirties, he was a handsome man, and with his black curly hair, dark eyes and swarthy skin he had the look of a gypsy about him.

'You've been let down time and again by the men in your life,' he told me, his voice deep and confident. 'You were married, but it was no marriage at all. You are alone now but it is not yet clear to me whether he died or you just wished him dead.'

I gasped and whispered, 'How did you know?' and he just smiled and said, 'I'm not here to judge you, just to tell you how it is or how it was. He was not good to you or for you and you deserved better. He had and still has his own lessons to learn.'

Continuing, he said, 'There is a younger man, very close to you. He lost his way for a while and caused you many problems, but is on a new path in life. You need have no worries. He will not let you down again and certainly not in the way he has in the past.'

'Thank you,' I murmured. 'It's what I've hoped for.'

'There has been a makeover of sorts and many changes have been made recently to your life and to you. The biggest change is in you. After allowing life to happen to you for so many years, it is as if you are now in control of your own destiny and the rest is up to you.

'You have been through a lot, but have come through it all a stronger person with a mind of your own. We are all here to learn lessons and yours have been harder than some but the worst is behind you now.'

'Thank you, that's good to hear.'

'Your family is about to grow and you will not be on your own for very much longer and then you will finally understand the meaning of true love. It will be with someone you already know but are not yet sure of. You may be surprised and perhaps have not thought this particular liaison would be possible. In the days to come I can see you driving a smart car with confidence, visiting a foreign country and living the sort of life that once you could only dream of.'

'Really?' I smiled a little doubtfully.

'Really,' he insisted so firmly that I had no choice but to believe him.

'Well,' Max questioned when I stepped blinking into the sunshine, 'are you going to meet a handsome prince and live happily ever after?'

I slipped the audio tape recording into my coat pocket and agreed, 'Yes, it was something like that, but he was pretty good. I'm glad I went in. Thank you for waiting.'

'No problem, but I'm afraid I've eaten all of the candyfloss.' Max waved an empty stick and screwed up his nose, 'It was more sickly than I remembered from my childhood, but I suppose we always look back through rose-tinted spectacles.'

Not me, I thought, but I am looking forward through them and, if the young man was right, I certainly had a lot to look forward to.

'I'd better get you home,' he said then, 'so that you can get ready for your visitors. Do you see a lot of your son?'

'Not as much as I used to, but that's for the best of reasons, because he's busy living a fulfilled life now and not coming to tell me about his latest scrape with the law.' I put a hand to my mouth, 'Oh, that sounds terrible, but I don't think Peter is any different from a lot of youngsters of his generation.'

'Mmm, I know Denise used to have her concerns about Jason, her son-in-law, but they appear to get on like a house on fire now. I can't say I was squeaky clean in my youth either. It took me a lot longer than it should to realize that honesty really is the best policy if you want to get on in life.'

'Didn't you and your wife ever want children?' I asked, adding, 'but don't think you have to answer that. Feel free to tell me it's none of my business.'

'The short answer is, no, neither of us

wanted children. Both too selfish for the kind of dedication it takes to bring up a family. I guess we valued our freedom too highly.'

'Well, at least you're honest and anyway too many people have children for all the wrong reasons and then no one is happy. Were you married very long?'

We had walked back to the car by this time and the indicators flashed as the doors were unlocked and Max opened the passenger side to let me in.

'Twenty-four years,' he said, 'and a half — we didn't quite make it to twenty-five.'

'That's a long time,' I commented, and climbed into the car, giving him time to tell me more, or not, as he chose.

As he drove out of the car park and filtered into the traffic, Max prompted, 'Aren't you going to ask me what went wrong?'

'You'll tell me if you want me to know but, yes, I was wondering, since you've asked.'

'She changed her mind about having a child but I didn't, so she found someone else to create a family with.' When I remained silent he asked, 'Nothing to say or temporarily shocked into silence?'

'A bit of both, I think,' I admitted.

'You're the first person I've told the real reason to. Even Denise and Adam were only ever given a watered down version of the facts.'

'Adam would certainly understand, since he went through something similar with Lisbet.'

'But with no baby involved — just a fitness trainer, as I recall.'

'I don't really know what to say,' I admitted, 'apart from, I'm sorry. You must have been devastated.'

'I made the mistake of not taking her warnings seriously, so I only have myself to blame.'

'Would it have made any difference if you had?'

I thought I had never seen anyone look as sad as Max did when he admitted, 'Yes, I think it might, because I loved her, you see. I would have done just about anything for her.' He glanced at me, and said wryly, 'I've never spoken about this before, but you're very easy to talk to.'

'Well, I'm glad,' I said and meant it, 'because keeping stuff bottled up does no good. It always helps to talk.'

'Do you want to talk to me, then?' he encouraged. 'I can be a pretty good listener when I try.'

'Not today,' I said firmly, 'because we're nearly home and it will take more than a few minutes to tell you the highlights and lowlights of my life. Perhaps some other time.'

'I hope there will be another time, hopefully more than one. I promise not to bare my soul every time, but I have enjoyed today.'

'Me, too,' I said and knew that I really meant it. 'You have my number.'

I was later home than I'd intended, but I knew the flat was immaculate thanks to my efforts that morning. There appeared to have been no more sightings of Jack, or Edna would surely have waylaid me, and there was no sign of Greg either and no answer when I tapped his door on the way up.

I kept the meal simple, with poached salmon, new potatoes and fresh vegetables. There was a sauce to serve with the fish but it was ready-made from a jar. I somehow thought Petie's girlfriend, this Lizzie, might be vegetarian, so many young girls were these days I'd noticed, and had thought fish was a safer bet for that reason. If not, even I could whip up an omelette.

There wasn't time to change but I'd just finished freshening my make-up and brushing my hair when the doorbell went. Pinning a bright smile on my face I rushed down the hall, and had thrown the door wide open before I realized who was standing there.

Faced with my worst nightmare, time didn't so much stand still as go rushing backwards — to a time I would far rather have erased from my memory.

# 14

I don't know how I managed to fight the urge to slam the door in my ex-husband's hatefully and surprisingly still familiar face, but somehow I did it. I had to get rid of him — and quickly — before Petie arrived and found him there, and to do that I had to gain and keep the upper hand. Reminding myself that Jack had no right to be there on my doorstep helped.

'Can I help you?' I said it coolly, as if I were talking to a stranger, which of course was exactly what I *was* doing.

Jack's bearded jaw dropped comically, his eyes popped under the black raised brows. 'Jo?' he said, 'is that you? My God, I do believe it is. What have you done to yourself? You look so . . . so different.'

I carefully ignored his comments. 'What do you want, Jack, because whatever it is, you'd better make it snappy because I'm expecting guests, but then as I recall you did always pick your moments.' My tone was clear and confident, I was pleased to note, and I was satisfied my tightly clenched fists and shaking legs were not evident to his searching gaze.

'Don't be like that, Jo,' he wheedled, 'aren't you even a little bit pleased to see me?'

The audacity of the man took my breath clean away, but I refused to let that rile me. I'd allowed Jack to get the better of me too many times in the past but this time it was going to be different. 'Is there any reason why I should be?' I queried flatly. 'The kindest thing you did for me in all the years of our marriage was to leave me. I would appreciate it if you would repeat that performance, quite frankly, and bugger off back where you came from. I have nothing at all to say to you and can't believe you would have anything to say that might be of interest to me.'

'I was hoping we could talk.'

'Didn't you hear any of what I just said? Only I *can* repeat it if that will help.'

'I'm asking you to spare me a few minutes. Is that too much to hope for?'

Conscious of the time getting on and the increasing chance of Petie and his girl arriving, I had to think fast. The clatter of Edna's letterbox made up my mind. 'You have no right to ask anything of me, but if it will help to get rid of you I will agree to spare you 'a few minutes', though it's more than you deserve and more than I want to give. Meet me tomorrow, midday, in the little park down the road. I take it you do remember where that is?'

'Yes, I do — and thank you.'

The next moment he was gone and I was left standing in the doorway and wondering if I had just dreamed the whole strange episode.

Edna's letterbox closed and the door opened. 'He finally found you in, then?'

'You don't miss a thing, do you, Miss Gutheridge?' I said and, stepping inside my own door, I closed it smartly.

My legs were shaking so badly that I had to lean against the wall for a moment and the mirror opposite reflected back a woman who suddenly appeared a lot older simply because of the haunted look on her face.

For the first time in my life I actually understood the meaning of the expression, 'I need a drink'. Going to the kitchen I reached to the back of the corner cupboard for the medicinal brandy bottle my mother had always insisted on keeping. It had been sitting there untouched for years but I was guessing spirits didn't deteriorate with age.

I wasn't sure what size portion a unit might be so I guessed and doubled it when I poured. Almost throwing the dark liquid down my throat in the desire to feel calm again, I immediately started coughing as it burned a fiery trail down my throat. Trying to catch my breath took all of my concentration and that alone made the exercise a success as I gasped and mopped my eyes.

Once I'd recovered, I did feel better, if a tad light-headed, and then I was annoyed to think I'd let Jack bloody Farrell get me into such a state. He had no right to just turn up unannounced and I should not have let his mere presence affect me in such a way, not after all these years.

The doorbell rang shrilly and I jumped and dropped the glass I was holding. Luckily, it fell into the sink and didn't break, so I left it there, and thrust the brandy bottle back into the cupboard, where I vowed it would stay, whatever crisis arose in the future.

It was a decision I was to regret almost immediately when I opened the door to reveal Petie standing beside an extremely heavily pregnant female of roughly around the same age.

I don't know how I hid my shock at the advanced state of her pregnancy, but somehow I managed to smile and say brightly, 'You must be Lizzie. Do come on inside.'

As I ushered them both in, I heard Edna's letterbox snap shut, which was inevitable, really. She must be having an absolute field day today, I thought ruefully.

'Do you want to sit in the lounge?' I encouraged Lizzie and an unusually silent Petie through, explaining as I went, 'Everything for the meal is ready to cook and it won't take very long. Are you all right with fish, Lizzie? Only I wasn't quite sure if you might be vegetarian or something.'

'Fish is fine and I'm not vegetarian or anything.'

I realized Petie was looking at me strangely, and then he suddenly said, 'Are you all right, Mum, because you look as if you've seen a ghost?'

He didn't know how close he was, thank goodness, and I realized I would have to tell him sometime soon about Jack's reappearance, but not yet, because we clearly had other — quite urgent — things to talk about.

'I'm absolutely fine so it's either my new foundation or I've skimped on the blusher,' I insisted, in what I hoped was a jocular tone. 'Now make yourselves comfortable, I won't be long.'

Petie followed me into the kitchen and wandered around as I put the vegetables and potatoes on and the fish ready to microwave.

'The flat's looking great,' he commented. 'Between the two of you, you've done a great job. How is Greg?'

'He's fine,' I replied, feeling quite guilty

because I didn't really know that for sure. I quickly assured myself it was good that we were both suddenly so busy and that I was sure to see him soon.

I was just about to encourage him back to the sitting room, where he'd left the poor girl on her own, when he reached the sink and picking up the glass he sniffed it, raised his eyebrows and said, 'Brandy. That's not like you, Mum.'

I was about to say — well exactly what I wasn't quite sure — when he got the wrong end of the stick entirely and asked, 'You haven't got yourself into a state about meeting Lizzie and this whole situation, have you?'

'I am concerned,' I admitted, which was no more than the truth, especially given what looked to be an almost full-term pregnancy which I'd assumed was only in the early stages. 'You have to allow that I'm entitled to be but, Petie, please go and sit with Lizzie. It's a bit rude to leave her in there sitting on her own. I'll call you if I need a hand, but I've purposely kept it simple.' I was relieved when he did what I asked.

'This is lovely, Mrs Farrell,' Lizzie smiled at me, quite shyly, tucking in with a great show of enthusiasm. 'I don't very often eat fish unless it's from the fish and chip shop, but this is delicious.'

'Mum doesn't often eat fish unless it's from the fish and chip shop,' Petie informed her cheerfully. 'She hates cooking now she's got no one else to cook for, don't you, Mum.'

'Yes, thank you, Peter,' I gave him the look I'd used to give him when he was a little boy and had overstepped the mark, even though I was quite sure it hadn't worked for years. 'I'm all right as long as I keep it simple,' I told Lizzie, encouraging, 'and please call me Jo.'

I liked the girl, I decided, as we ate and chatted about this, that, and everything, but nothing about the subject we were here to talk about. I guessed her age to be around twenty-four or twenty-five. She had long blonde hair, streaked with other colours, and it fell straight and silky to her shoulders. She was quite tiny except for the almost incongruously enormous baby bump that some sort of stretchy dress only seemed to emphasize.

After fruit salad and ice cream, both shop bought, we moved to sit more comfortably and I served coffee.

Petie embarrassed me by demanding, 'Why are we drinking out of fiddly cups instead of mugs, Mum? You don't have to put on a show for us, you know.'

Lizzie endeared herself to me even more by telling him, 'Stop it, Pete. Your Mum has never even met me before and I think it's really nice of her to make an effort. Thank you, Jo, and the meal was lovely.'

'You're welcome.' I smiled, and then brewed myself up to ask, 'Am I allowed to ask when the baby is due, Lizzie?'

'Of course you are, you can ask anything you like. The baby is due in three weeks.'

'Oh, my goodness,' I was shocked and made no attempt to hide it, 'as soon as that.'

'You haven't known very long, have you?' she asked quite kindly, and I shook my head.

'Well, I haven't really known that long,' Petie put in. 'Have I?'

They looked at each other for a long moment and, sensing tension, I wondered what was coming next.

'I didn't know myself for quite a while,' Lizzie turned to me, obviously deciding I was the one deserving of an explanation. 'I was almost three months gone before I did a test. I think I was in denial, but once I knew I realized I would have the baby no matter what. Pete and I weren't seeing each other any more by then, and I assumed he would want me to have an abortion, so I didn't tell him.

'I know that was probably wrong of me,' she hurried on before anyone else could speak, 'but I wasn't thinking about Pete at that time, just about me and the baby.'

'I can understand that,' I nodded, 'because I did much the same thing when I found I was expecting Peter. My marriage was hanging by a thread by then and I was pretty sure that having children was not in Jack's plan — and certainly not with me.'

'You never told me that.'

'He was actually excited when I did tell him.' I felt I should point that out, in fairness to Jack.

'He didn't stay excited for very long. In fact, he didn't stay.' Petie didn't sound upset and we both knew it was just a statement of the truth. 'It has a lot to do with him that I was so reluctant to get involved when Lizzie did tell me about the baby. I thought I might turn out like him, in which case the baby — and Lizzie — would be better off without me.'

'Oh, Petie, you're nothing like your father and good or bad parenting skills are not inherited, they are learned, mostly as you go along. I've always hoped I did better than my parents with you, even though I had to do it mostly on my own.'

I looked at him questioningly because I knew we'd had our moments in the past, especially when I pushed him out of the nest and forced him to take responsibility for his own life and his own behaviour.

'You,' he said, with his youthful face very serious for once, 'have always been the best Mum in the world, far better than I ever deserved. I've told Lizzie all about you, haven't I, Lizzie?'

'I can't believe he was such a nightmare,' she marvelled, her blue eyes wide and wondering. 'How on earth did you put up with him?'

'With difficulty at times, believe me,' I said with feeling, adding, 'but you'll learn, Lizzie, as the years go by, that your child is always your child. Whatever they say and whatever they do cannot and will not change that. I just hoped that if I stuck with it, Peter would turn his life around. He has and so it's all been worth it.'

'You really love him, don't you?' Lizzie asked the question softly, and I replied, without hesitation, 'Oh, yes.'

'But does loving a child come more naturally to mothers than to fathers?' Petie asked, with a frown. 'After all, the mother carries the child and gives birth, so the bonding process must begin that much sooner.'

'Mmm, that's a difficult one,' I admitted, 'especially because I haven't had that much experience of decent fathers. I can't even cite my own as a good example, but that doesn't mean there aren't any. What about yours, Lizzie?'

'I can't help, I'm afraid,' she grinned ruefully, 'because mine took off before I was born. My stepfather is OK but I don't feel that close to him.'

'What about Rob?' I remembered Denise's late husband with a surge of real relief. 'He was a great dad to Bobbi.'

Even Petie looked relieved. 'Oh, yes, he was, and at times he was like a dad to me, too. Even though he must have got sick of my bad behaviour, he always turned up at the court to speak up for me and he never, ever turned his back on me.' He looked sad for a moment. 'I wish he was here to see me now.'

'And what about Adam? Look how he's taken both you and Bobbi under his wing — and Jason, too, come to that — and he's not even a biological dad at all. Actually,' I said, remembering, 'Bobbi bought Rob a mug once and the words on it said, 'Anyone can be a father, it takes someone special to be a dad'.'

'Isn't that lovely?' Lizzie blinked rapidly and, looking straight at Petie, she told him, 'You can be someone special if you want to be.'

'Thanks,' he nodded, 'I would like to be a

good dad to our baby.'

I looked from one to the other of them. 'Does that mean — ?'

Petie understood what I was getting at right away and quickly put me straight. 'We're not together, Mum. Not a couple any more. It just means that I can be a good dad and Lizzie a good mum, whatever our relationship and personal circumstances.'

'Of course you will be,' I said stoutly but I was bitterly disappointed and I freely admitted it, if only to myself. I was sure Petie had said he loved Lizzie. They would make a great couple and, selfishly, for both the baby and for me, I wanted them to be a family. Still, I consoled myself at least this baby would have a mum *and* a dad, unlike Lizzie and Petie.

'We'd like you to be part of the baby's life, Jo,' Lizzie leaned towards me. 'We might not be able to provide a granddad between us but two great nannies might be some compensation for that.'

I'd been afraid to ask — to expect — and now suddenly my heart was full and so were my eyes. Tears dripped onto my clenched fingers and it felt as if a huge weight had been lifted from my shoulders. The thought that somewhere a grandchild of mine would be growing up without me being involved in any way had been too difficult to even contemplate.

'Is there anything I can do, anything I can get for the baby? I'm afraid I don't knit.'

'Well, thank God for that,' Petie breathed a huge and heartfelt sigh of relief. 'I don't want any son of mine dressed in woolly jackets and bobble hats. Those old photos of me are frankly embarrassing.'

'It might be a girl,' Lizzie pointed out, laughing, 'and you can get whatever you like for the baby, Jo. I'm just happy that you've been so great about this pregnancy being dropped on you and that you want to be involved.'

Petie looked on bemused as the two of us planned a shopping trip, and one we decided should take place sooner rather than later because there obviously wasn't much time to waste. It wasn't until they left sometime later that I realized I hadn't given a thought to the child's paternal grandfather or taken a moment to warn Petie that he was back.

I hoped the oversight wasn't something I was going to live to regret.

# 15

I didn't sleep much at all for a second night, which I actually thought was hardly surprising given all that was going on in my life after a fallow period lasting several years where nothing much had happened at all.

I could hardly complain, I thought, when I had been all for bringing change into my pretty humdrum existence. The list I had come up with originally, on that first evening spent in Greg's company, now seemed fairly tame when compared to the reality that was currently spicing up my life.

In the space of just the last twenty-four hours three unbelievable things had happened. First of all, a very attractive man had brought me flowers, taken me out to lunch and expressed real interest in seeing me again. Then, my very ex-husband had turned up on the doorstep out of the blue and, if I *were* looking for a positive side to that, it would be that I felt I had handled the situation firmly and with confidence and was sure I could continue to do so. Finally, and best of all, I could now really start looking forward to welcoming a precious grandchild into my family.

Reining in my enthusiasm for the latter, I accepted that for the moment I had to put my mind to this meeting with Jack. Had I been given a choice, I would have told him to get lost in no uncertain terms the minute he turned up at my door. However, he had caught me wrong footed with the arrival of Lizzie and Petie imminent and my main objective had understandably been just to get rid of him as quickly as possible. God knows what would have happened if they had all come face to face on my doorstep. I don't think *I* could have coped, never mind Edna.

I had no appetite at all for the scrambled eggs in front of me, and pushed the fluffy mixture around the plate in a desultory fashion as I wondered what on earth Jack could possibly want from me, because he surely wanted something or he wouldn't be here.

I wish I had said I would meet him earlier because, as it was, I had hours on my hands to speculate and worry, and I was already doing so as the eggs and cup of tea, still untouched, and stone cold testified — and then I got annoyed.

He couldn't do this, just walk back into my life as if nothing had happened, causing all this turmoil but, as I finally realized, I was the only one allowing it to happen. I told myself over again, but with more force than before, that he had no control over me — not any more — and with that thought firmly in mind I went to get ready.

Pride made me make an extra effort with my appearance. I didn't *want* Jack back — God forbid! — but that didn't mean I didn't want him to see what he'd been missing all these years. He wasn't to know that the big change in my appearance, my home and my life was only very recent. I had also come to realize and accept that looking nice and feeling good about myself boosted my confidence levels no end, and I was sure I would need to keep a tight grip on all the confidence I could get when dealing with a man who was a past master at draining every bit of mine away.

I didn't want to look as if I had gone to a lot of trouble on his account, but still chose casual clothes that flattered me. I wore jeans, but they were white, a long sweater in a deep coral — the sort of colour I would once never have dreamed of wearing — and my make-up was lightly but meticulously applied, just as the lady in the shop had showed me. The sweater and the silvery tone of my hair gave my complexion a warm tinge and, giving my reflection a brisk nod, I squared my shoulders. Ready to take on anything, never mind an ex-husband I didn't give a fig for, I picked up my bag and headed for the door.

I was, of course, far too early, so I took myself for a brisk walk well away from the park, and with every step I felt calmer and more certain of myself.

Even so, I almost jumped out of my skin when a car pulled up right next to me and a voice said, 'Where are you off to in such a hurry on a Sunday morning?'

I stared at Greg as if I'd never seen him in my life before, feeling strongly as if I'd been caught with my hands in the till, metaphorically speaking. I couldn't tell him about Jack and my half-truths, not out here on the road, just like that, and minutes before I rushed off to meet the very man. How on earth would that look, for heaven's sake?

I suppose he felt he had to speak, seeing as how I remained awkwardly silent, and so he said, 'I wasn't being nosy, I just wondered if you wanted a lift.'

'Erm.' I struggled and eventually blurted, 'Actually, I'm meeting someone and I'm almost there, but thanks anyway.'

'Oh, OK.'

I felt I had to say more and rushed on. 'I would like to have a chat, Greg. I shouldn't be too long. I could pop in on my way back if you're going to be home. If not, just let me know when it would be convenient.'

He gave me a puzzled look. 'It's always convenient for you to call. We're friends, Jo. You're welcome any time. Perhaps see you later, then,' and with that he was gone, leaving me looking after him feeling worse than I would have thought it possible to feel and bitterly regretting keeping him, of all people, in the dark about my true marital status.

I could see Jack in the distance the minute I walked through the park gates. He must have been there some time because he was pacing back and forth in a great show of impatience, continually checking his watch with a deep scowl on his face, which became more pronounced as I approached unnoticed. He'd never had a single patient bone in his body and I knew I wasn't late.

Then he saw me, and the change was nothing short of miraculous. His bearded face creased into the most charming smile he could muster. I had seen that same smile used to devastating effect over the years on any member of the opposite sex he'd deemed worthy of his attention. He'd very rarely wasted it on me once we were married and it did absolutely nothing for me now. I refused to smile back.

Jack came right up close to me and it was

all that I could do not a take a step back. 'I thought you weren't coming,' he said taking my hands into his and looking right into my eyes.

'I'm not late,' I pointed out, fighting the urge to wrestle my hands away, letting them lie limp in his instead. 'Now, what did you want to see me about, Jack? My time is precious, as I'm sure is yours, so say what you have to say and we can go our separate ways just as we have been doing all these years.'

'So cold towards me,' he said sadly.

I raised my eyebrows. 'What exactly were you expecting, Jack, a warm welcome, open arms, the fatted calf? If you were, I'm afraid you're going to be sadly disappointed.'

'Look,' he said pointing, 'there's a café over there. Can we at least sit down and talk over a cup of tea?'

My immediate instinct was to refuse, to tell him just to spit it out, whatever was so important that it couldn't be dealt with in a letter or over the phone but must be said face to face.

He saw me hesitate and rushed on, 'We can be civilized, can't we, Josie? All I'm asking is ten minutes or so of your time. You owe me that much.'

It was the wrong thing for him to have said and I could tell from his face that he realized it instantly, but before he could say another word, I told him, coldly and flatly, though with great emphasis, 'I owe you *nothing*, Jack. Do you get that? I owe you nothing at all.'

'Sorry, sorry.' It was the first apology he had ever offered to me, and it was many years too late in coming. 'Please be kind enough to share a pot of tea with me, while I tell you why I'm here.'

'Very well.' Anything to get this over with, but the tiniest satisfied twitch of his lips irked me no end. Jack had always taken great pleasure out of getting his own way.

The place wasn't crowded, and while Jack went to the counter I took the time to look around. I knew I was checking, almost nervously, to see if I knew anybody, which was plainly ridiculous. I could drink tea with whomever I liked on a Sunday morning — or any other morning, come to that. I was, after all, a free agent. Even so, I made my way to a table tucked away in the far corner and waited in some trepidation for Jack to join me so that I could discover the real purpose of his visit.

We sipped tea, he ate a biscuit, and on the surface it was all very civilized, but I just didn't want to be there in my ex-husband's company and there was no doubt in my mind that Jack was very nervous. Since he'd had the upper hand throughout our marriage, however, I wouldn't have been human not to be amused by the fact the shoe was very much on the other foot today. That was the reason I fought the urge to tell him just to get on with it, and waited patiently for him to work up to whatever was bothering him so much.

'How is Peter?' he asked.

I looked at my watch and commented, 'It's only taken you the best part of an hour to ask how your son is, Jack. But as you've shown no interest in him since the day you left, I suppose I shouldn't be surprised.'

'You know we thought it was best to make a clean break.'

'I know that's what *you* thought, I don't recall that Peter or I were ever given a choice in the matter.'

Jack had the grace to look uncomfortable, and he shifted in his seat.

'This is ridiculous,' I said when he appeared to have nothing to say, 'I don't have the time or the inclination to be sitting here exchanging niceties with you, Jack. Either say what you've come here to say or I'm leaving.' As if to prove the point, I stood up and reached for my handbag.

'All right, all right,' he said hastily, half

rising from his chair. 'Please sit down. Shall I fetch more tea?'

'I don't want your company and I don't want your tea. In fact, I can't believe anything you have to say will be of any interest to me, I only agreed to meet you — '

'So that I wouldn't bump into Peter on your step,' he guessed, adding, 'I saw him arrive. Who was the pregnant girl with him — his wife?'

'None of your damn business,' I replied smartly, but I was shaken to think he had hung around in order to check out my visitors, and horrified that he might have stepped right out and introduced himself to an unsuspecting Petie. 'What were you doing, spying on me? How bloody dare you?'

'No such thing,' he protested rather too hotly and I knew instinctively he was lying.

I sat down. 'Five minutes, Jack, and then I'm leaving, walking away, just as you did all those years ago.' I crossed my hands primly in my lap and looking him right in the eye, I waited for him to start which, with a bit of huffing and puffing, he did.

'I've changed,' he said continuing quickly when he saw the sceptical expression that I made no attempt to hide, 'I no longer drink or even smoke. I'm a man of means, Josie, and I want the chance to make up to you and

Peter for what I put you through. I know,' he went on when I opened my mouth to interrupt, 'that I don't deserve that chance and I can see you've managed just fine without me, but I'm asking anyway.'

'You . . . you,' I struggled to get the words out I was so angry, 'have no right, no bloody right at all, after turning your back on me and your little boy — *especially* your little boy — to waltz back and expect to pick up the pieces of family life just like that. You can just bugger right off back to wherever you've been and whoever you've been with all these years.'

The audacity of the man almost took my breath away, but then I'd lost count of the times during our marriage that he'd disappeared on a bender with my housekeeping money or been caught with his hands in some barmaid's knickers and he'd always — yes, always — been able to talk me into giving him another chance. I could hardly blame him for trying this time, and he *might* have changed, just as he'd said, the difference was that this time so had I.

'I let you both down badly,' he said, in the biggest understatement I'd ever heard, 'but I've come back in the hope that I can make it up to you if you will just give me the chance to try.'

'What chance did you give us? Tell me

that.' I demanded, absolutely incensed. 'The boy you left is now a man, the woman you left is a lot older and a hell of a lot wiser, Jack. You can't turn the clock back and erase those years however much you want it. You were a lousy father and an even lousier husband and we learned to live without you so well that we've never even missed you for one minute.'

'You're right. You're absolutely right. Everything you say is no more than the truth, but surely everyone deserves a second chance. I'm not asking you to take me back, Josie, though if you did I would be the happiest man alive. Just let me be part of yours and Peter's life again. Let me show you the man I can be — the man I *should* have been.'

I'd listened to enough, enough to know when I was being conned. Too many things didn't ring true and this whole big show of fake sincerity almost made me physically sick.

'The answer,' I said, standing up again, and this time determined to remain on my feet, 'is *no*. It's way too little and way too late. I don't know what your game is, Jack, but don't try to make Petie and me a part of it, because it won't work, do you hear me?'

I hear you,' he said sadly, 'and I wish I could change your mind, but obviously I have to accept your decision.'

Well, that did surprise me. Jack accepting anything I said without an argument was a first. I felt relieved, and was quite ready to wish him well in his changed life before I went back to mine, but he wasn't finished yet.

'What about Peter?' he gave me a straight look. 'Is he to be allowed to make his own decision? As you so rightly said, he's a man now and should be given the choice of whether or not to welcome me back into his life.'

'You leave my son out of this,' I said sharply.

'He's my son, too,' Jack pointed out.

'Since when?' I demanded. 'Certainly not for the last God knows how many years, and certainly not when it came to paying for his keep. Where were you when he was ill? Where were you when he was in trouble? Where were you when he needed a father? Nowhere to be found, that's where.'

'Say it all, Josie, say it as it is. It's all true. Everything you can throw at me I accept, because I know it's no more than I can deserve, but is Peter to be denied this chance to know his dad because you can't forgive me my past misdemeanours?'

# 16

The rest of the rather more than one-sided conversation was a blur to me, but one thing remained crystal clear in my mind long after I had walked away, leaving my ex-husband sitting there at the café table with a well-remembered smug expression on his face. I had no choice. If I didn't tell Petie that Jack was back in the area and wanted to see him, then Jack would do it himself.

Everything I had achieved recently suddenly meant nothing. The newly found confidence I had built up so laboriously week-by-week had been undone in the space of one hour of Jack's company. I had laughingly believed the power had shifted, that the new me could deal with anything he might throw at me, but I had foolishly forgotten one thing — that he was well aware of my Achilles heel, and that was Petie.

I consoled myself that he didn't know where to find Petie, but only briefly, realizing almost straight away that all he had to do was to keep turning up to where I lived and eventually their paths would cross. Many years too late I cursed my reluctance to move away from the marital home, but it had just seemed wiser at the time not to uproot Petie when his father left. Added to that, the flat was a good size, situated in a good area, the rent had always been reasonable, and eventually I'd been given the opportunity to buy.

In those first moments, as I walked away from Jack, I thought of moving out immediately, or of telling Petie he could no longer visit me. Surely a reason would be easy enough to come up with. I even, in my panic, thought of moving abroad and taking Petie with me. Common sense prevailed fairly quickly with the latter one, since it just wasn't possible to emigrate overnight anyway, and I knew Petie would never go for it. His life was finally sorted, with secure employment prospects and his baby's birth practically imminent.

I stopped, feeling my shoulders sag with the weight of the inevitable. As always, Jack had won, because he knew I had no choice but to tell Petie the truth and leave it to him to make up his own mind whether he saw his father or not, and I had only a few hours in which to find a way to do it.

I needed a friend in that moment more than I had ever needed one in my life, but there was no way I could turn up on Denise's step in the middle of a family weekend she had been looking forward to for weeks.

I felt as if the cares of the world were on my shoulders as I dragged my heavy feet up the stairs towards a home that had recently been the cause of so much pride and pleasure but, sadly, no longer felt like my haven.

I did pause on the landing outside of Greg's door and was so tempted to knock I even raised my hand, but I was trapped by my own lies, or half-truths, which amounted to pretty much the same thing. I remembered the awkwardness between us earlier that morning and turned to continue my journey up the final flight.

I heard nothing, no door opening, no word was spoken, but the hand touching mine where it lay on the banister was the most welcome thing in the world at that precise moment.

Too upset to even cry, I allowed Greg to lead me into his home. Making sure I was comfortably seated, he found a rug from somewhere, which he tucked securely round me, and went to turn up the gas fire. Only then did I realize I was shaking so much that my teeth were chattering alarmingly.

He made tea, holding the cup to my lips while I sipped the hot, syrupy, sweet brew and felt the welcome warmth course through my body.

'Thank you.' I think I managed a wan smile, because he smiled gently back. 'You must wonder what on earth's the matter with me.'

'It won't hurt me to wonder.'

'Before I can talk about what's happened this morning, I need you to know that I've misled you. Not purposely,' I hastened to add, 'and not by telling a downright lie about me, and my circumstances, but by not correcting an assumption you and possibly a few other people will have made about me. I hope you will be able to forgive me.'

'Jo,' Greg came to sit beside me, taking my cold hands into the warmth of his, 'I thought we'd agreed it wasn't necessary to know *everything* about one another to be friends. I know enough about you to know that I like you very much and I don't think there's anything you can tell me now that could change the way I feel.'

'Even if I tell you that the person I was going to meet this morning was my ex-husband. Ex-husband, you will note, not *late* husband as I led you to believe.' I hung my head, too embarrassed to look Greg in the eye. I didn't need to remind myself he deserved better from someone he looked upon as a friend.

Greg took one hand away from mine and I was bereft as I waited for him to remove the other. He didn't even want to touch me, and who could blame him? He was obviously repulsed by me and that was no more than I deserved.

One finger was placed under my chin and it tilted my face up until I was looking into kind blue eyes, filled with the sort of understanding I'd never in my wildest dreams expected from him.

'If this is what an hour in his company does to you, Jo, I can't even begin to imagine what years of marriage to him might have done to you. I think it might be perfectly understandable that you preferred to think of him as dead. In fact, though, I don't believe you ever actually said what had happened to him, and I'm quite certain I never asked.

'Now, if you're feeling better, do you want to talk about what happened this morning? You never know, I might even be able to help, though my present instinct is to simply punch him on the nose the very next time I see him. I take it he was the tall, rather arrogant guy who came calling when I was decorating your flat.'

I nodded glumly, and admitted, 'I just don't know what to do, Greg.'

'He wants you to take him back?' he hazarded a guess.

'Saying no to that was the easy part,' I admitted, and feeling the rush of weak tears to my eyes, I blinked rapidly. 'He wants to see Petie. I refused, and he was quite right when he said that wasn't a decision for me to make.'

'Surely Peter won't want to see him after all this time? From what I gather he's had nothing to do with the boy in years, and I would think Peter would find that hard to forgive. I know I would if I were in his shoes.'

'You don't understand,' I told him, not adding that I could barely understand myself, but going on to say, 'when Jack left, I did things, said things, to make it easier for Petie — who *was* very young at the time — to accept that he had gone, without feeling rejected or thinking it was in any way his fault. Which children are apt to do, you might know. I made every excuse under the sun for Jack. One of the things I said was that he'd had to go away to find work so that he could send us money to live on.'

'And did he?'

'Well, he might have got work elsewhere, who knows? But we certainly didn't see a penny of it.'

Greg swore, which I had never heard him

do before, and he shook his head in patent disbelief. 'How did you manage?'

'It was around the time that my father died. My mother didn't want to live alone and I couldn't manage to work full time and look after Petie without help, so she moved in with us and solved both of our problems.'

'But I thought you never got on with your mother. I'm sure you told me — '

I smiled without humour. 'You don't forget much, do you? It wasn't easy.' Only I knew what a massive understatement that was. 'I knew she had no time for me, and that never changed, but she adored Petie. He was the apple of her eye, and it meant he never came home to an empty house. Between us, we built up this huge pretence and practically made Petie's father into a saint in his absence. I've never actually told Petie his father is — or at least was — in reality, a drunken womanizer who would literally and quite happily take the food from his son's mouth.'

'You must tell him,' Greg stated flatly. 'He's a man now and deserves to know the truth, however unpalatable.'

'No.' My tone was emphatic and that's when I knew I had made my decision. 'Petie is older now and he's not stupid, he's worked out for himself over the years that Jack wasn't a great husband or father, but whatever Jack is or was, he is still Petie's father and I never want him to feel ashamed of who he is or where he came from. I have to tell Petie his father is back and let him make up his own mind about how he deals with that.'

'He's a bright lad,' Greg sounded confident. 'He'll see through him in a minute.'

I shook my head. 'You don't know my ex-husband. He's convinced that nothing is ever really his fault and is equally as good at convincing others the same thing. He's also very good at getting his own way.'

I heaved a great sigh and asked if we could change the subject. Greg went along with that immediately, offering to cook lunch while I read the paper, an offer I was only too happy to accept. For a little while life almost felt normal as we talked about the cake decorating classes, which I thought aloud that I might discontinue. Given my aversion to cooking, this seemed only sensible.

'I'll miss you being there, though,' Greg said kindly, before I pointed out there were any one of half a dozen ladies in the class only too eager to step into my shoes and my place at the next table to keep him company.

'I will definitely keep up the driving lessons, so I don't intend to give up on the list entirely. Talking of the list, did I tell you I went to a clairvoyant and had a reading yesterday?'

Greg gave me very sceptical look. 'And?' he said, obviously showing interest because he felt he had to, but with reluctance.

'Let me see if I can recall the highlights,' I found myself smiling, in spite of the traumatic events of the morning, 'because I can tell you're desperate to hear all about it.'

He grimaced, but encouraged, 'Go on, then.'

'He, the guy who did the reading, seemed to know all about my marriage and even about the problems I used to have with Petie. He even said he wouldn't let me down like that again.

'He said I wouldn't be on my own much longer, and would fall in love with someone I already know but hadn't thought of in that way before — or something like that.'

'Oh?' Greg showed a tiny spark of interest. 'Any idea who that might be?'

'Well,' I decided it was a time for honesty, 'I have been seeing someone. Actually, that's a slight exaggeration, I have seen someone, but only the once, and that was yesterday.'

'Ah,' Greg nodded, 'the guy with the flowers. I did wonder, and no, I haven't turned into Edna, but you can't help noticing some of the comings and goings when you're pottering around during the day. Nice car.'

'Nice guy, too, as far as I can tell from my second and third impressions. My first impression was that I wasn't keen,' I added, without elaborating, except to say, 'I met him through Denise and her husband.'

'Good luck with that, then,' Greg looked happy for me, which I thought was generous of him, seeing that falling in love was on his list but not on mine.

'I'm sure it will happen for you soon,' I consoled. 'You could have your pick of the ladies at the icing class. They know a great catch when they see one.'

'Thanks for that,' he laughed, 'but I'm keeping my options open for the time being.'

'No one in particular in your sights then?' I couldn't help probing, thinking how nice it would be to see Greg settled with someone.

'That would be telling, now, wouldn't it?' he tapped the side of his nose, 'But you'll be the first to know if and when I tick off number one on my list. Now, anything else from this clairvoyant?'

'Mmm, he said he could see me driving.'

Greg looked impressed in spite of himself. 'I have to say, it doesn't sound like the usual twaddle that gets dished out when you hear about these things. I might go there myself. No,' he went on hastily, 'I was only joking.

That sort of thing is definitely not my cup of tea, but he seems to know his stuff.'

'Time will tell, and I have an audiotape in case I forget what he said. Shame he didn't predict the ex-husband returning or I could have asked him what the outcome will be. He did say I'd learned some hard lessons, but that the worst was behind me now. I think I will hold on to that and trust that he's right.'

'More tea?'

'No,' I stood up and folding the rug I placed it neatly on the couch. 'Thank you for everything, Greg, I don't know what I would have done without you these past weeks and especially today. I'm going upstairs to ring Petie now. I will tell him only that his father wants to see him, and leave the rest up to him.'

'For what it's worth, I think you're doing exactly the right thing — probably the only thing in the circumstances.'

My steps were lighter as I made my way up the flight of stairs between Greg's flat and mine. In all honesty, although I hadn't given Jack much of a thought in years, I felt it was almost inevitable that he would turn up like the bad penny he was. If it wasn't now it would probably be at some far more inconvenient time in the future, so best get it over with.

If everything worked out and he and Petie became friends, then I must be big enough to accept Jack's appearance was better late than never and be happy for Petie.

'Don't put off until tomorrow what you can do today,' I told myself sternly when I had thoughts of putting the kettle on first, or just watching the news before I made the call, and my voice sounded loud in the silence of the flat.

I noticed my hand shook as I reached for the receiver, and when it rang before I could even lift it, I felt as if I had leapt a foot into the air and my heart was literally crashing against my ribs.

In the seconds before I picked up, I convinced myself it might be Jack, showing his usual impatience and already getting on my case. I had already formulated my reply, which would be along the lines of: 'Don't bloody bully me. I'm no longer the wife you used to push around and I will do this in my own good time.'

Then, I suddenly realized — hoped — that it might be Max and snatched the receiver up before he could get bored and hang up.

'Hello.' I sounded breathless, girly and eager even to my own ears and cursed myself for not playing it cool.

'You sound a bit puffed. You shouldn't be running up those stairs at your time of life.'

'Oh, Petie, it's you. How lovely to hear from you.'

The initial relief at hearing my son's voice vanished as quickly as it came, once I remembered that I had been about to ring him — and why.

'It hasn't been that long,' he joked, 'I only saw you last night. I just wondered how your weekend has been and what you thought of Lizzie.'

'I thought she was lovely,' I said warmly.

'Yeah, I thought you might like her. She's pretty cool and so are you actually, Mum, for being so accepting of our circumstances.'

'Well, the days of shotgun marriages are long gone, thank goodness,' I said with feeling, 'and I guess your situation isn't so very unusual these days. I'm just glad that you intend to be involved, for the baby's sake, and very happy that I am to be included in his or her future.'

'A little bird tells me you had a date yesterday,' Petie teased, 'I hope you didn't get back early on our account.'

'It wouldn't matter if I did,' I told him firmly. 'Family will always come before friends.'

'Is that what Max is then, a friend?' he pried shamelessly.

'After one 'date', as you referred to it, I should certainly hope so.'

'Good catch for my Mum,' Petie said bluntly, 'he's rolling in it.'

'You should know by now that money doesn't impress me,' I told him sharply, 'and I believe he's a bit of a one for the *younger* ladies, so I shouldn't get your hopes up, Petie.'

'I just want you to be happy,' he insisted honestly, 'and you can just as easily be *rich* and happy. I know he's been around the track a few times since his divorce, Mum, but I have it on good authority that this time he's smitten, so you've obviously made a great impression. Anyway,' he laughed, 'I think I've wound you up enough about your love life for now, so I'll leave you to it.'

I was about to say goodbye, when I realized I hadn't told him that I'd been about to ring *him*.

'Petie, just a minute, there was something I wanted to talk to you about. In fact, I was about to ring *you* when the phone rang.'

'Oh, right. What was it, then?'

'Erm.' I found myself hesitating, searching for the right words, and the phone line hummed quietly as Petie waited, and then I said, 'There's no easy way to say this, Petie, so I'll just have to come right out with it.'

'There's nothing wrong, is there, Mum? With you, I mean?' The concern in his voice was immediate and heart warming.

'No,' I said, hurrying to reassure him, 'but . . . I've had a visit from your father and he wants to see you.'

# 17

The silence following my bald statement was deafening, and it was so lengthy that I wondered if Petie had even heard what I said.

'Did you hear me, Petie?' I asked anxiously. 'Your father is back in the area and is keen to see you.'

'Is he indeed?' Petie's voice suddenly exploded in my ear. 'If he's so bloody keen to see his son, why has it taken him so long to remember I exist?'

It was a question so typical of Petie and one that so deserved an answer that I almost applauded. Whatever Petie decided, I thought, Jack wasn't in for an easy ride. I even had it in me to feel a little bit sorry for him — but only a little bit.

'I can't answer that,' I pointed out, 'but I said I would pass on the message.'

'Will he be seeing you again?'

'Probably not, but then it's not me he's come to see. We're no longer married, but he is still your father.'

'But not in any way that counts,' he said with bitter truth. 'What do you think I should do?'

'You can't ask me that, Petie. It's

something only you can decide. He has no rights, and you should remember that, but you have every right to see him. I have to say you would be pretty unusual if you weren't at least curious.'

'Mmmm,' he sounded undecided.

'Look,' I said, 'I'll leave it with you. I'm sure this has been a bit of a shock.'

'You can say that again,' he interrupted. 'One hell of a shock.'

'I have his phone number, which I can give to you now, or I can give yours to him. Whichever you think best.'

'OK, give me his number and I'll have a think about it.'

'You do that,' I encouraged and reaching for the piece of paper with the number scribbled on it. I read it out.

'Mum, will it upset you if I *do* decide to see him?'

'No, my son, it won't upset me,' but even as I said it, I wasn't sure if I was telling the truth or not.

I had only just replaced the receiver when the phone rang again and this time it was Jack demanding, without preamble, 'Have you told him yet?'

'It might surprise you to hear me say this, Jack, but I am no longer here just to do your bidding.' I was proud of my strong tone and even stronger words. 'As it happens, Peti-er,' I corrected, knowing that Jack would ridicule the pet name for our son that he had always hated, 'phoned *me*, so the answer is, yes, I have told him. He has your number and it's up to him whether or not he chooses to use it.'

'You had better — ' he began.

'Don't you bloody *dare* threaten me,' I said, slamming the phone down so hard it was small wonder it didn't break into a dozen pieces, but perhaps they made the instruments these days strong enough to withstand slamming, I thought without humour.

When it rang again immediately, I snatched it up furiously and barked, 'I thought I told you — '

'Christ, I hope I never get on the wrong side of you,' Max laughed so hard he almost choked.

'Sorry, I just had a nuisance call,' I excused myself, calming down so quickly that I felt a bit like a deflating balloon as the hot air whooshed out of me.

'Dare I even ask if you've had a good day?'

I screwed up my nose, even though I knew he couldn't see. 'We-ell,' I said thinking of Greg and his kindness, 'it wasn't all bad.'

'And the meal last night?'

Oh, yes, I remembered, that was when it

had all started, with the visit from Jack just before my genuine visitors were due to arrive.

'The meal was fine and I found out I'm going to be a granny,' I found myself smiling at the thought.

'Good God,' he sounded shocked, 'you don't look anywhere near old enough. Are you pleased?'

'I'm thrilled,' I said firmly. 'Now, how was *your* day and your evening?'

'Nothing special without you to share it, I found. I had a great time with you yesterday. I really enjoyed it and I hope you did, too.'

'Oh, I did, and the flowers are still gorgeous, thank you, and the bear, of course.'

'Ah, yes, the bear,' he said, and something in his deep tone made me shiver deliciously and imagine all kinds of possibilities. 'Now, how soon can I see you again?'

'How soon would you like to?'

'Tonight? Tomorrow night?'

I fought the urge to just tell him to come on round right away. As much as I would have liked to, I was all too aware he probably had quite enough eager women on his case. Added to that, I knew I wasn't looking my best after the long emotional day I'd had and I did want to look my best for a man like Max.

'Tonight is out,' I told him without giving a

reason, 'I have a class tomorrow evening and a driving lesson the following night. I could manage Wednesday, if that's any good for you?'

'I suppose it will have to be,' he sounded gratifyingly disappointed. 'I was flying to Manchester on business on Wednesday morning, but it will just have to wait until Thursday.'

'Oh, you don't have to put it off for me,' I protested.

'Believe me, I *do*.'

★　★　★

Denise was waiting and pounced the minute I got into work on Monday.

'What on earth have you done to our Max?' she demanded, all agog. 'He turned up at lunchtime on Sunday, quite obviously expecting to find you there and his disappointment was palpable when he realized you had other plans. He ended up staying to lunch, of course, and didn't stop talking about you the whole time. We all found it absolutely hilarious.'

'Oh, Denise, it was your weekend with the family. It was a bit thoughtless of him to come barging in on it like that. I even thought twice about making my phone call, and that was practically an emergency.'

'Yes, tell me all about that *and* about your date with Max. Hang on, I'll ask the temp, it's another new one by the way, to make some coffee. She might be able to manage that, in between filing her nails.'

She was suitably horrified at Jack's off-hand and extremely demanding attitude after years of absence and neglect of his son, and she was suitably impressed with Max's determination to take me out again sooner rather than later. It was fair to say that very little work got done through the morning by the time I had also heard about the visit from her daughter, son-in-law and cherished granddaughter.

Denise's battles over recent years almost immediately following the loss of her beloved husband, Rob, had to be heard about to be believed. With her family dumping all their problems on her one by one, it was a wonder she had survived, never mind turned them all around in order to get on with her own life. Starting with her mother's decision to walk out on a long and — one would have assumed — happy marriage, there had quickly followed her daughter's decision to give up on the nursing career she had previously been so determined on.

As if that wasn't enough, there was the

added complication of the prospective son-in-law from hell living with them all in *her* home and then her daughter's unplanned pregnancy thrown in. The whole experience had been a lesson to me in how things could turn out right in the end, against all expectations. That being the case, I set all of my hopes on the same sort of happy ending being a possibility for me.

'I think you're right to leave it all to Pete,' she said firmly. 'That boy has a good head on his shoulders these days. You know Jason sees his father now and again?' I nodded and she continued, 'The relationship between them can never be perfect, unfortunately, but he does have a better understanding of his father's past behaviour these days.'

'And his mother?'

'Ah, well, that's a similar scenario to Pete's with his father, since she saw fit to take herself off to the other side of the world and leave the boys to the mercy of a father whose parenting skills were ropey to say the least. There's very little contact there; an occasional letter is about the sum of it. At least Pete has always had you, and no one could fault your parenting skills. He's a credit to you, and only you, since you were the one who stood by him, quite literally, through thick and thin.'

'You stood by a boy who wasn't even yours,' I pointed out, referring to Jason, in whose eyes Denise could do no wrong.

'Families, eh? Sometimes we can't live with them and yet we can't live without them.'

'I could live quite happily without one member of mine,' I said with feeling, 'although, strictly speaking, he's no longer a member, and not much more than a bloody nuisance at the moment. Petie has enough on his plate with becoming a father shortly himself. He can well do without his own father deciding he will suddenly become one after years of opting out.'

'Leave it to Pete to sort Jack out,' Denise advised again. 'You've made huge changes to your life and to yourself. I've never seen you as happy or as confident as you've been lately. Please don't let that waste of space spoil everything for you. You've always deserved so much better and now, finally, you are getting it. What's on your busy schedule for tonight, anyway? I love it that you've kept Max waiting for another date, I don't think that's ever happened to him before. You, my lady, are playing a very clever game.'

'It's not a game,' I protested, slipping my jacket on as the clock on the wall counted down the seconds to home time. 'I'm going to cake decorating tonight, though I've decided not to keep it up. It's fun, but not really my thing, but it seems rude to leave so soon without saying anything to the tutor about why. Though it's actually my loss and not hers, since I've already paid for the term. Greg will keep going,' I added, and will probably be quickly snapped up by one of the other ladies as soon as my back is turned.'

Denise surfaced from retrieving her bag under the desk. 'And how will you feel about that?' she asked, looking mildly curious.

'I'll be thrilled to see Greg settled into a happy relationship again,' I insisted. 'Why on earth wouldn't I be?' But even as I said it, I wondered how something like that would affect our friendship and felt a distinct pang of regret at the thought of losing something that had come to mean so much. 'I'll be over the moon,' I said, more forcefully, and turning to go I said over my shoulder, 'See you tomorrow. We might get some work done then.'

I tapped Greg's door as I passed on my way up the stairs to my flat. He seemed surprised when I said I would be going to the class after all, but thought my reasons were commendable.

'I haven't had time to make anything so I picked up a cake from the bakery as I was leaving Cheapsmart. I thought that would illustrate the point that I wasn't really into cooking.'

'Good thinking,' he agreed, 'though I've kept a spare in the freezer for you, just in case.'

'Oh, Greg, that is good of you. I'll remember that when I get unexpected visitors. I'll call for you on my way down later.'

'You do that. I think we should go in the car tonight because rain has been forecast for later and it's quite a stride there and back.'

'Lovely. You can talk me through the gear changes, because when and why is still a complete mystery to me.'

'I'll look forward to it.' He was chuckling away as he closed the door, and I was still smiling at the sound as I closed my own.

I felt like changing, freshening my make-up as I did so, and flicking my hair to give it a bit of height. Show those old biddies at the cake decorating what they had to live up to, I thought, because some of them obviously thought Greg and I were a couple. I hoped whoever got him handled him with care because he was a gentle, even quite shy man, and some of these more mature women could be quite desperate once they got their claws into a man. He'd run a mile, I imagined, if one of them pounced on him, and the thought made me smile.

I saw them looking down their noses when I brought out my shop-bought cake and I couldn't have cared less, though once it might have embarrassed me. They obviously had more time and more inclination for homely pursuits, which was fine for them. I was evidently one of the few working women in the class. Most appeared to be widowed or divorced with both time and money on their hands.

Gillian, who worked on the next table to mine, couldn't quite hide her delight that I was leaving, though the tutor professed herself sorry, which was nice of her since I was convinced she had one eye on Greg for herself.

Really, I thought, they were like a lot of vultures circling their prey and I felt more than a little nervous about leaving Greg to their tender mercies. He would need to have his wits about him if he was to survive.

'Can I watch you making those rose petals, Greg?' Gillian sidled across and squeezed in between us, with a sly look at me. 'You have such wonderfully light hands and make it look so easy. My efforts look so clumsy in comparison to yours.'

I looked at my own lumpy flowers and then

at her delicate and very realistic buds and hid a smile. Honestly, he was like a lamb to the slaughter, I thought, as he went through the creative process with her in exactly the same way the tutor had done not half an hour before.

'Oh, you are clever, Greg,' she said admiringly, standing so close you wouldn't have got a piece of greaseproof paper between them. 'I don't know how you do it.'

'Well, it's quite easy if you take your time.' He obviously didn't know when he was being taken for a fool, I thought quite crossly, as he offered, 'I'll go through it with you once more, shall I?'

Greg soon had a little crowd of simpering women around his table, cooing in admiration and vying for his attention, so I took my puny effort to the tutor for some tips on improvement just because she was looking po-faced and extremely redundant.

In the car on the way home I bit back a few acid retorts about Greg's harem, telling myself it wasn't really his fault, he was just too nice for his own good. From his own comments he just thought everyone was being friendly or genuinely did need his help and was totally unaware of his own appeal. I reminded myself, quite severely, that it was none of my business, even if I was of the opinion that he was worth better than the likes of Gillian what's-her-name who, by the look on her chinless face, had the grim determination to see off the competition.

I worried again momentarily about how he was going to cope without me there to protect him. By his own admission he'd led a pretty solitary existence since he'd lost his beloved Monica and hadn't been out in the big wide world for very long at all. The thought almost had me deciding to continue with classes I really had no interest in — which was plainly ridiculous — and above and beyond the call of the duty of a friend.

I couldn't quite see the appeal myself and took a sly look at him from the corner of my eye, trying to see the attraction. You could do worse, I supposed. He did drive a nice car and own his own flat, and he wasn't bad looking now he was making a bit of effort with his appearance. I supposed he could be looked on as quite a catch, *if* he was your type. I rather regretted that he wasn't mine but knew that he never would be, not in a million years. I had someone very different in mind.

# 18

After giving up on the cake decorating classes, I was rather pleased when I went for my next driving lesson that Derek professed himself more than happy with my improvement behind the wheel, even though, as he said himself, it was still early days.

'You don't think I'm one of those women who should never be allowed on the road, then?'

He laughed and shook his head, 'No, really, Jo, you're doing fine and the nerves must be improving. I do believe you've actually stopped shaking when you climb into the driving seat.'

I thought about what the clairvoyant had said and wondered what kind of car I would end up driving. Something small, I sincerely hoped, and certainly not too expensive. Perhaps a Ford Ka or a Vauxhall Corsa, because either would suit me, though the prospect of taking to the streets on my own was daunting, to say the least. Still, I was sure that time, and a lot more driving tuition, would change that.

'Why don't I put the L-plates on this?' Max

offered as we set off in his car the following evening. 'Not right now, obviously. I would need to put you on the insurance first.'

'But it's a BMW, isn't it? It might get damaged. Aren't they very expensive?'

'Jo, it's a car. I was planning on letting you drive it, not crash it.'

I was horrified. 'I'm not even very good yet.'

'And you won't be unless you practice.'

'It's really kind of you, but — '

Max seemed to lose interest then and just said, 'The offer's there, just let me know if you change your mind.'

I was worried that I'd offended him, but by the time we reached the restaurant he'd chosen he seemed to have forgotten all about it. It was a place I'd heard a lot about from Denise and I recalled her describing it in great detail after one of the few dates she'd gone on before she'd settled down with Adam. The menu, she had grimaced, was all in French without subtitles, and the prices, she'd assured me had, without a word of a lie, made her eyes water.

I couldn't fail to be impressed as Max ushered me inside and we were shown immediately to a table within one of the high-sided booths that took up the centre of the restaurant, with normal tables around the outside.

To my relief, the long dress and little shrug I wore had been exactly the right choice. I was glad now that I'd taken my time and I consoled myself it wouldn't take too long to put away all the items of clothing I'd tried and discarded when I got home.

I wasn't going to pretend it was the sort of place I came to all the time, so I told Max honestly that my French had never been up to much, and that I was happy for him to order for us both, as long as he didn't pick snails or frogs' legs which, I was happy to agree, were probably delicious but just not for me.

'One of the things I like so much about you is the way you never try to put on airs and graces. I find it totally refreshing.'

'You'd have seen through me in a minute,' I assured him, 'especially when I ordered the service charge. That would have been a dead give away.'

He roared with laughter and I saw the couple opposite glance across and then do a double take. The woman leaned forward and peered at me more closely in the subdued lighting. 'Jo, is that you?'

'Pauline?' I suddenly recalled her from the pub the night Greg and I had gone out for that drink together, right at the start of our individual makeovers. It seemed like a million years ago. 'And Keith, isn't it? How are you both?' I suddenly remembered my manners, 'Oh, excuse me, this is Max.'

Max behaved impeccably, insisting that they join us, though there was really no need since they could hardly even be classed as friends, and he acted the perfect host. He even ordered champagne and Pauline's eyebrows flew higher than the cork when it popped at such extravagance.

'Haven't seen you at the pub since that night,' she told me chattily, 'though we've bumped into Greg a couple of times. Don't you see him any more?'

I laughed and explained, 'I actually see him all the time because he lives in the flat beneath mine. We're just good friends.'

'That's what they all say,' Keith said snidely and with a suggestive wink. I wanted to hit him.

'In this case it's the truth,' I told him firmly.

'How long have you two been seeing each other, then?' Pauline asked, and I wondered if they were always this nosy. I knew I wouldn't have dreamed of asking personal questions about their life.

'Not long enough or often enough,' Max said firmly, adding, 'but that's something I intend to put right. We met through friends.'

'Do I take it that love is in the air?' It was Keith again and he was beginning to seriously get on my nerves.

'It's far too soon to tell and you're embarrassing us both,' I told him bluntly.

⋆　⋆　⋆

'I felt like telling him to save his breath to cool his soup,' I told Max later when we were in the car and driving home. 'I do apologize, but they really aren't friends of mine. I've only met them once.'

'Ah, yes, when you were out with this Greg. I think I've heard Denise mention his name. Should I be worried?'

'About what?' I turned in the passenger seat to stare at him.

'Exactly how good a friend is he — or if you want me to come right out with it, do I have competition?'

I was mystified, and couldn't think what on earth he was getting at. 'Competition? Competition for what?'

'For your affections, to put it the old fashioned way, my lovely Jo, because though I really like you I wouldn't like to think I was treading on anyone else's toes.'

'You must think I'm in great demand, so I'm flattered, but I am a free agent and

Greg *is* only a friend.'

'I'm relieved to hear it.' Max brought the car smoothly to a halt outside my block of flats, and turned to look at me. 'I would like to see a *lot* more of you, preferably without your nosy friends, because tonight was fun but it wasn't quite what I'd had in mind for this evening.'

'Really?' I stared up at him, all big-eyed and with totally false innocence, and found him staring right back at me.

'No,' he said deeply, 'not what I had in mind at all.'

I knew he was going to kiss me and part of me wanted that so badly, while another part wanted nothing more than to leap out of the car and race to the safety of my own four walls. It felt like a million years since I'd been in a man's arms, especially a man who obviously had designs on my body. Then his mouth was on mine and I stopped thinking and definitely stopped worrying as I melted into his arms.

Perhaps not quite a million years, but it *was* a very long time since I'd been kissed — and I was pretty sure I have *never* been kissed like that in my life before. When Max released me I was dizzy with longing, and long-forgotten emotions threatened to over-whelm me.

'Wow,' he said, and all I wanted at that moment was for him to kiss me again. Without me saying a word, he quickly obliged, with a growing urgency his tongue probing my lips in a way that was intimate beyond belief.

I'd forgotten what it was to want a man sexually because there had been no one in my life since Jack had walked out. I'd forgotten how it felt to be a woman head over heels in love and desired by a good-looking man. It made me feel beautiful and unbelievably alive. I wanted him to touch me intimately and I wanted to touch him, to make him feel as good as he was making me feel.

Pulling away slightly, he looked at me in the darkness of the car and asked with a trace of urgency, 'Aren't you going to ask me in?'

I wanted to, more than anything I wanted to. I wanted to lie in his arms, to welcome him into my body and to know again the almost forgotten pleasures of the flesh.

I fought a battle with myself, and I finally won, realizing it would be too much too soon, especially with a man like Max, who was very experienced and probably far too used to getting his own way. I didn't want to be just another notch on his bedpost or a tick in his blackberry. Some things were worth waiting for — and I had a feeling that sex with Max would be one of those things.

'Not unless you want a coffee,' I told him, 'because that's all that's on offer tonight.'

He looked disappointed but, even in the darkness, I could swear I saw a deepening respect in his eyes. He kissed me a chaste goodnight at my door and turned to look at me one more time, before leaving.

Once I was inside, my initial regret turned to relief when I saw the state of my bedroom and realized how mortified I would have been to have had to put off the scene of seduction while I cleared the discarded clothes scattered across my bed.

There would be another time — hopefully many of them, I consoled myself — and if it was going to be as good as I thought it would be between us, I knew the first time would be well worth waiting for.

I hung the redundant clothes away, already planning what I would wear the next time, and blessing Denise's forethought when she'd insisted I buy all new underwear. Staring dreamily at my reflection in the mirror was like looking at someone I didn't even know, I acknowledged. Who was that slim, elegant lady with the faraway gaze?

The sharp ring of the telephone snapped me out of my reverie in a moment and I told myself a call at this time of night could only be bad news. Unless . . . I paused before picking up the receiver and wondered if it could be that Lizzie had gone into labour and the baby, my grandchild, could be on its way. I felt a thrill of excitement that doubled and then trebled when I heard Petie's voice sounding bright and happy at the end of the line.

'Met him,' he was saying, and I realized it must be a baby boy. No wonder he sounded so thrilled because most men hoped for a son, didn't they? Petie was gabbling on, and I couldn't really make head or tail out of it because he was talking so fast.

'It's a boy, then?' I interrupted. 'The baby?'

'The *baby*?' he laughed, and his voice sounded high and young. 'I'm not talking about the baby. I'm talking about Jack . . . my father.'

# 19

'You've seen — ' I faltered.

'Yeah, Jack ... my dad ... although he prefers me to call him Jack,' Petie confided brightly, ' 'Cos, as he said, we'll be more like mates really.'

He continued happily in the same vein, more about what they said and what they did and, as he talked, all the good feeling I had come home with drained out of me. I told myself not to be selfish, to try to be glad for my boy because he was obviously so happy to have his father back in his life — and I truly was — but I couldn't get rid of the feeling that all was not what it appeared to be. I decided there and then, as I listened to Petie, that if Jack let him down again I would kill him, probably slowly and painfully.

'I'm glad for you ... both,' I said when Petie paused, obviously expecting some kind of response.

'I knew you would be and that's what I told Jack. He wasn't so sure because he knows his track record isn't great, but he thought it would be a good idea if we all got together, you know, as a family.'

'A fam — ' I couldn't say any more and almost choked on the word. Jack didn't even know the bloody *meaning* of the word as far as I was concerned. Yet he could waltz back into his son's life after an absence lasting almost the *whole* of that life and have the audacity to think he could stick us all back together because it was what *he* had decided he wanted right now. With my suspicious mind, I could only wonder why.

'Yeah, a family again, Mum. Wouldn't that be great?' He paused, obviously waiting for me to say something and when I said nothing, he rushed on, 'Oh, I know it wouldn't be the same and that you won't be getting back together or anything — although I get the feeling Jack would love that more than anything — but we can all be friends, can't we?'

What else could I say but, 'Of course, we can.' Not for Jack, because I owed him nothing at all, but for the son I loved more than anything in the world. I owed Petie at least that much for making the wrong choice of father for him, because he had deserved so much better. Anyway, if Jack had decided to be a father to him at last after all these years and it was what Petie wanted, who was I to object?

Denise, pretty predictably, didn't agree when I spoke to her about it while we were on our lunch break the next day. 'Fair enough if Pete wants to see him,' she said, 'but I don't see why you have to get involved in their bonding sessions.'

'You have to see it from Petie's point of view,' I insisted. 'He doesn't ever remember a time when we all lived together and — '

'And whose fault is that?' she demanded crossly. 'I don't recall you being given a choice when Jack decided to take himself out of your lives. He was never the best husband or father, and he probably did you both a huge favour by buggering off when he did, but he didn't have to disappear off the face of the earth, did he? Hasn't he ever heard of access visits?'

'Well, that's all a bit hypothetical now, isn't it? He's back and I have to deal with that the best way I am able.'

We both chewed on our cheese salad sandwiches and thought about the situation, and then Denise asked the question that had been bugging me for days.

'Yes, he's back, but *why* is he back, Jo?'

I shook my head. 'Who knows? Not me and not Petie, as far as I can tell. A fit of conscience, starting to feel lonely now he's getting older, just plain curious to see how his son has turned out — you tell me.'

I could see she didn't buy any of my suggestions, but Denise refrained from further comment, except to say bluntly, 'What a pity you didn't move house years ago, because then there would have been nothing for him to come back to.'

I didn't disagree, but I didn't agree either, even though I very much wanted to. I found Greg was much more sympathetic when I spoke to him about it but, in fairness to Denise she did know far more about my circumstances and my life, having known me so much longer. It was, however, still comforting to have someone appear to understand my reasons for agreeing to a meeting I had absolutely no stomach for.

'I don't see how you can do anything else, really,' he said, though even he didn't look entirely happy about the situation I found myself in.

'You don't?' I felt relieved at his response, because that was exactly how I felt.

He shook his head. 'It's not actually that much for Peter to ask, is it? It's only natural he would like to see his two parents in the same place at the same time. Most kids would take that for granted and have photos of their family together going back years. I know that's not always the case, and your circumstances are not unusual, but ask the children and most would say that's what they wanted. The trouble is, their wishes mostly get overlooked when things get acrimonious between the parents.'

'Thank you so much,' I said, close to tears.

'For what?' Greg looked puzzled.

'For seeing my point of view.'

'Jack should be thanking you,' he pointed out, 'from the bottom of his heart, if he has one, for the fact that you are seeing this from Petie's point of view, because the way I see it is that he's the one who really counts.'

Unfortunately, that wasn't the way Max saw it when I had to say I couldn't see him on Friday evening because that was when this 'family get-together' had been arranged for.

'Playing happy families, Jo?' he almost scoffed at the thought. 'It's a bit late for that, surely? Why on earth would you want to meet up with your ex-husband after all these years, unless — '

'I'm doing it for my son,' I cut in swiftly, 'and for no other reason.'

'Because?'

'Because he's asked me to.'

'He has no right to ask such a thing of you.' Max sounded outraged.

261

'He has every right.' I was equally indignant. 'He's my . . . our . . . son, and the fact we messed up is not his fault.'

'Your son is a grown man now,' he pointed out, his voice cold, 'he hardly needs you there to hold his hand.'

'Well, that's your opinion,' I told him, 'and you are, of course, entitled to it. You don't have to agree, but you do have to respect that it's something I feel I must do, and whether I want to or not, doesn't come into it.'

The telephone call ended on a frosty note with no arrangements for another date even hinted at. I was absolutely gutted. Max was the first man I had been interested in for years and now it looked as if I had blown it. I couldn't blame Petie, and I never would, but it was very hard not to heap the blame on Jack, who seemed to have come back into my life for the sole purpose of screwing it up all over again.

The flowers that turned up to work the next day were a surprise and a relief. They were totally gorgeous, red roses in a veritable cloud of gypsophila, and the temp was agog as she placed them on my desk and said in barely concealed amazement, 'These are for *you*.' Even Denise did a double take when she came in the door.

'Forgive me,' the card said, the writing a

bold and black scrawl, 'I should have been more understanding. I'll ring you. Max.'

I was thrilled, forgave him instantly and tried to ignore the slight niggle that insisted that, yes, he should have been a lot more understanding.

The second bouquet, when it arrived around lunchtime, was an even bigger surprise and, I thought, a bit over the top even for someone like Max. White roses, this time, with white freesias, and the temp was almost beside herself.

'Well, I'm jealous now,' Denise looked indignant. 'I've *never* had more than one bunch of flowers in a day in my life. I *told* you Max was totally smitten. All these must have cost an absolute fortune.'

'I've only had flowers from the petrol station,' the temp said in a peeved tone. 'It's a good job they're already in water, or they'd all be dead by the time you got home.'

'And I think I'd better give you a lift,' Denise was laughing now, 'because you'll never get them home in one piece otherwise.'

I found I was laughing, too, when I reached for the second card, but the moment I read it all traces of a smile were wiped from my face. I held it out to Denise, who took it, read it and then threw it on the desk in disgust.

'Remembering the good times and looking

forward to seeing you tonight,' it said, 'yours, Jack.'

'Who's Jack?' the temp asked curiously, reading the card from where she stood, and then she wandered off, losing interest when no one enlightened her.

'Oh, dear,' Denise pulled a face, 'I have a horrible feeling he's reading way too much into the fact you've agreed to meet up.'

I didn't respond, I was too busy staring down at the beautiful white flowers and remembering. What did surprise me was that Jack had obviously remembered, too. I was touched that he had, and I really didn't want to be.

'I think so, too,' I said quietly when I looked up and found her watching me. 'These were the flowers I carried on our wedding day.'

I was still subdued when Max phoned later and apologized all over again, and I think he thought I was still miffed with him.

'I was just jealous,' he said honestly, sounding quite unlike his usual confident self.

I forced a laugh, and said, 'You, Max, jealous?'

'I can't compete with Jack, can I?' he said surprisingly. 'You have a history and a child together.'

'Yes, we have,' I agreed, feeling flattered in

spite of myself. 'We're also divorced and have been for many years. It's Peter Jack is interested in, not me.'

'I wonder,' Max said, and I wondered, too, as I looked at the snowy flowers that couldn't help but evoke long ago memories of happier times before it all went so horribly wrong.

★ ★ ★

The evening that followed was one of the strangest of my whole life, being the first I had ever spent in the company of my grown-up son and my very ex-husband. How could it not evoke feelings of what might have been? And Petie's obvious joy at being part of a complete family was strangely infectious. I would have felt like a complete party pooper had I not joined in with Jack's 'do you remember when . . . ?' from Petie's very young years.

'I filled the kitchen sink and let it run over while you were both asleep?' Petie looked at me. 'You never told me that, Mum.'

'It went through the ceiling of the downstairs flat,' Jack grinned, his bearded face alight with enjoyment, 'and I had to go down and apologize and offer to redecorate.'

Actually, as I recalled that particular episode, I was the one who apologized and offered to pay for any damage, but I didn't want to seem as if I was nit-picking, so I remained silent, telling myself it was just a detail.

Jack had brought us to a very nice restaurant, held my chair before the waiter could do it and insisted we have whatever we liked from the extensive menu.

'Did you like the flowers?' he asked, as he filled my wine glass yet again.

'Flowers? You bought Mum flowers?' Petie looked so delighted that my heart sank, especially when Jack pointed out the significance of his choice of blooms.

'I used to buy your mother flowers all the time when we were first married,' Jack recalled, not altogether accurately, adding as if he were an expert. 'Roses were always her favourite.'

'I thought they were daffodils,' Pete accused, 'that's what you've always told me.'

'Daffodils *are* my favourite,' I said firmly, pointing out, 'my taste in flowers has changed over the years.' As has my taste in men, I might have added.

I couldn't truthfully have said I didn't enjoy an evening I had actually been dreading from the minute I agreed to it. The food was delicious, Jack was at his most charming and, best of all, Petie didn't stop beaming from the time I climbed into Jack's car and joined the two of them.

I couldn't fail to notice the envious looks I got from the other ladies in the restaurant and I'd have been a fool if I hadn't realized why. We looked like the perfect family group, because there was no doubting how like his father Petie was, though thankfully only in looks. Both men were undeniably handsome and focusing their attention on me throughout the meal as if I was the most important woman in the world. Only I knew that for one of them the huge show of affection was no more than a sham.

When Petie left us for a moment, Jack leaned towards me and placed his hand over mine. 'This,' he said regretfully, 'is the way it should always have been.'

I tried to move my hand away immediately, but he held it firmly and without an embarrassing struggle there was no way I could remove it from his grasp.

'Well,' I probably spoke more sharply than I intended, 'that would have been impossible since one of us wasn't around and you, of all people, Jack, should know that you can't turn the clock back. I should also add that I, for one, wouldn't want to. The years with you were *not* the happiest of my life and you must be well aware of that.'

'I want to make it up to you.' His brown eyes, always so deep and dark that you felt you could melt into them, were full of regret and for a moment I stared back at him wishing and wanting that for just one time in my life I could believe he meant what he said.

Then a champagne cork popped close by, and there was Petie laughing down at us, yelling, 'Surprise.'

I saw the look on his face and realized how it must appear to him. His mother and estranged father sitting close together, hand in hand and staring into each other's eyes like a couple of lovesick teenagers.

I wanted to shout, 'Nooooooooooooo. It's not what it seems at all,' but Jack kept my hand firmly in his and laughed into my eyes as he accepted the glass of champagne in the other hand. Raising it he chinked against the glass Petie put in my hand and said, 'To us.'

I could have been wrong — and I hoped with all my heart that I was — but it felt as if this was what Jack had intended all along. Finally, I managed to snatch my hand away but I knew it was far too late, because I had already seen hope and happiness blossoming in my son's eyes.

# 20

I didn't sleep a wink that night, something I seemed to be making a habit of. I felt trapped in a living nightmare where my life was turned on its head and I was back where I started from — in the nightmare of the marriage from hell.

No one, not a living soul, had ever known just how bad those years had been. Even Jack, who had been the cause of it, seemed to have either erased the misery he had caused from his memory or simply reinvented history.

Had Jack been alcoholic or simply a heavy drinker, had he been unfaithful throughout our marriage or was it, as he'd always insisted, all in my imagination? All I knew was that every bit of spare money, and often money that was already earmarked to pay a bill, was spent in bars where the barmaids knew Jack by name and practically sat in his lap right there in front of me on the rare occasions that I joined him.

Had I imagined that, though I was the only one working, I was also the only one who went without? I soon learned the hard way that if Jack didn't get what he wanted he gave me a hard time, sometimes a very hard time. Had I imagined the nights he stumbled home drunk smelling of another woman's perfume or worse, and the nights he didn't come home at all and couldn't — or wouldn't — explain where he'd been?

I miscarried our first child after hauling him drunk and incapable up the two flights of stairs to our flat one night. After that I didn't get pregnant for a very long time, and sometimes I was grateful for that, because my world wasn't one you would want to bring a child into.

Why I didn't just get up and leave is a question I asked myself many, many times, both at the time and since, and my reasons are the same ones you will hear from the majority of women living in similar circumstances.

I loved him and he always swore he loved me and would change, or alternatively he told me that no one else would ever look at me, and I believed him. I did think that I couldn't live without him and was convinced that he wouldn't manage without me because I did everything for him.

There were also just enough glimpses through the years of the charismatic man I had fallen in love with to keep alive the pretty unrealistic hope that one day he would return to me for good.

When Petie was finally born, my focus changed and he became the centre of my world. I do think Jack made an effort, at least for a while. I think he knew by then that what I was willing to put up with for myself, I wasn't prepared to put up with for my child. He even managed to hold down a job for a while so that I could spend time at home with our baby.

Gradually, though, I can only think the pretence all became too much for him and he reverted to type. I heard the rumours and covered my ears, saw the evidence and closed my eyes, but I didn't truly believe he would leave us — not until the day I collected Petie from school and came home to find all trace of Jack had been erased from the flat. It was as if he had never been there.

The only contact, until he had turned up on my doorstep a few days ago, had been the divorce papers that landed on my mat citing a separation of five years as the reason. I'd signed the papers with a flourish and a sigh of relief, thinking that was that. It just goes to show how wrong you can be.

I could accept that he had turned his back on me without a thought — people do fall out of love — but what I had always found impossible to accept was the way he had walked away from his son without an explanation or a backward glance. I was finding it equally difficult to accept the way he had walked right back into Petie's life and was now, so many years on, prepared to play the doting father. It just didn't make any sense and neither did his sudden interest in me.

As the light of dawn filtered through the curtains, from out of nowhere I suddenly recalled what the clairvoyant guy on the seafront had said to me and it brought me bolt upright in my bed.

*'You will not be on your own for very much longer and will finally understand the meaning of true love. It will be with someone you already know but are not yet sure of. You may be surprised and perhaps not have thought this particular liaison would be possible.'*

Oh, my God, my hand crept up to my mouth and remained there as realization dawned. He'd been talking about Jack, hadn't he? Not Max, as in my heart I had allowed myself to hope and dream, even though it was such early days.

He said Jack had lessons to learn and perhaps I should believe that some really had already been learned. Jack said he had given up the drink, and that had been the biggest problem in our marriage. Was that why he had come back, because he now had something to offer and wanted to make amends for his past behaviour towards us? It seemed unlikely, given his track record, but I supposed anything was possible, and he *was* looking very prosperous, dressed in his smart suits and driving an expensive car.

Perhaps he really had changed, after all, *I* had, and out of all recognition. Some days I felt like a different person entirely and that made me wonder why I found it so hard to give my ex-husband the benefit of the doubt and believe this particular leopard really had changed his spots.

In the end, I got up and threw back the curtains because going back to sleep was obviously not an option for me. I was on my way to the shower when the phone rang, making me jump and panic a bit about who on earth might be ringing at that time on a Saturday morning.

'I have a hot croissant fresh from the bakery down here with your name on it,' Greg said, with a smile very apparent in his voice. 'I just came back from the supermarket and noticed your bedroom curtains were already pulled back. Shall I pour your coffee now?'

'Five minutes,' I said. 'Give me five minutes to have a shower and I'll be down.'

The relief of not having to suffer my own unanswerable questions and hypothetical scenarios for another minute was palpable. Greg and his common sense — not to mention his croissants and coffee — were *exactly* what I needed.

After showering and finger drying my hair, I pulled on jeans and a T-shirt, paused for long enough to add the bare minimum of make-up, and tripped down the stairs. The clatter of Edna's letterbox distracted me just long enough to wonder if she ever slept, and then Greg was welcoming me in, chiding, 'Five minutes, my eye. Mind you,' he stood back to let me pass, and looked me up and down with an approving nod, 'it was obviously time well spent. You look good enough to eat along with the croissants.'

'Good God,' I pretended to swoon, 'was that a compliment, Greg Masters? Wow, I must be doing something right but, if I might say so, you're looking pretty dapper yourself. In fact,' I suddenly burst out laughing, 'we look like twins.'

We looked each other up and down. Blue jeans, white T-shirts, the only difference was that my top had a bit of feminine lace at the neck.

'Never thought I'd be comfortable in a pair of jeans,' Greg said gruffly as he pulled out a chair for me at the kitchen table.

'Me neither,' I admitted, pulling the butter dish towards me, eager to taste the croissant with my name on it. 'Now I have several pairs. I guess we both finally got dragged kicking and screaming into the twenty-first century. Mmm,' I stopped talking to enjoy the warm flakiness of the pastry, and the richness of the melting butter.

'So,' he said eventually, when we'd eaten two each and were on a second cup of coffee, 'how did it go last night?'

I honestly hadn't intended to tell him any of it, but I blamed him for asking when the whole thing, chapter and verse came pouring out.

'Quite an evening,' Greg commented.

'You can say that again,' I said ruefully. 'It's obviously what Petie wants, for Jack and me to get back together. What do you think? Is it Jack or is it Max the clairvoyant meant?'

'I think,' Greg began slowly, pausing to put more sugar into his coffee and then to take a sip.

'Yes, yes,' I prompted impatiently.

'I think,' he said again, 'that's something only you can decide.'

'Oh, Greg,' I felt deflated. 'I thought you

would have some words of wisdom for me.'

'Those,' he said, '*are* words of wisdom. It could equally be neither of them. Perhaps someone you know from work. And have you stopped for even a minute to think the clairvoyant might have been wrong?'

Greg was right, of course, on both counts, and I told him so. What I didn't tell him was that my heart had been set all along on it being Max. After all, who in their right mind wouldn't want a tall, grey-haired and utterly gorgeous man like that in their lives? Not me, that was for sure.

'How's it going with Gillian?' I asked to change the subject.

'Who?' Greg looked at me blankly for a moment.

'From the icing class,' I prompted encouragingly.

'Oh, yes, Gillian,' he said, and gave me a look. 'She phoned and invited me round to hers for a meal. How did she get my telephone number?'

I gave a sheepish grin. 'Erm, yes, that might have been me. She seems very nice,' I added, not all together truthfully, though I accepted that it was only my opinion.

'Yes,' he said, and didn't sound entirely convinced either. 'I'll be going round there later.'

'Well, that's good,' I said encouragingly, adding, 'I'll bet she's an amazing cook, and a lovely woman.' I stood up. 'Thanks for the croissants, coffee, and most of all for listening.'

'I'm sure you'll do the same for me when I have to make a decision about which woman to choose.'

'And it will happen,' I assured him, quite sure that it would because he was shaping up to be quite a catch in my eyes. 'Of course,' I added, 'when it does I shall tell you the same as you've already told me.'

'Which was?'

He'd obviously forgotten already, which was pretty amazing since it was hardly two minutes ago. 'That's something only you can decide,' I reminded him with a satisfied smirk.

'Oh, yes.' Greg screwed his nose up, and said, 'Not very helpful.'

'Perhaps not, but you were right. You usually are, I've found.'

He opened the door for me, and as I stepped out onto the landing he said, 'I wonder if Gillian knows I'm Mr Usually-Right.'

I was laughing my head off as I ran lightly up the stairs, and feeling so much better than when I had gone down. Funny how an hour in the company of someone sensible could make such a difference, but finding Max waiting on my doorstep hidden behind another enormous bouquet finished the job of making my day.

Without even thinking, I leaned around the flowers, kissed a freshly shaved cheek and laughing up into his face, I asked, 'Are you going to be making a habit of this?'

'If that's the greeting I get, I think I will. You look,' he said, his eyes warm and approving as he looked me up and down, 'good enough to eat.'

'That's what — ' I began, almost adding that it was what Greg had said and quickly changing it to, 'you think, is it?'

'Mmm,' he murmured, and nodding towards the door, asked, 'any chance we can go inside? Only I would like to greet you back and it's a bit public out here.' Edna's letterbox clicked shut and we both grinned.

The door had barely closed behind us before Max dumped the beautiful blooms unceremoniously into the hall chair and drew me into his arms with a groan of deep appreciation.

I gave myself willingly as his mouth claimed mine and realized immediately that something had changed between us. There was something about the way his tongue probed my lips that was intimate beyond belief. It felt, I realized, as if we were already lovers and I accepted it was only a matter of time before we were.

My pliant body was dragged hard up against him and I was left in no doubt at all of the state of his arousal, and a small involuntary moan escaped from my mouth and into his — and then the phone rang.

The harsh ringing was a dash of cold water to our overheated senses and we sprang apart as if someone had stepped into the room. Flushed, breathing heavily and looking distinctly ruffled, we stared at each other.

Then Max reached for me again and urged, 'Just ignore it.'

'I can't,' I said ruefully, 'it might be my son.'

'He'll ring back.'

'I have to answer it,' I told him, back in control. 'It might be important.'

'I'll put the flowers in water.' He looked disappointed, but then, with him not having children himself, I accepted he would probably never understand that being a mum was a twenty-four hour a day job, even when they were grown up.

'You sound breathless. Have you just run up the stairs?'

Jack's was the last voice I wanted to hear

and his tone chilled the remaining heat running through my veins in a minute.

Ignoring his question, I asked one of my own. 'What do you want, Jack?'

'It wasn't so much what I want as what you might want, like to spend the day with your husband and son.'

'*Ex*-husband,' I pointed out, 'and while I think it's commendable that you want to spend time with your son,' I carefully swallowed the sarcastic *at last* that was in danger of slipping out, and continued, 'I don't think it's at all necessary for me to be there, and I do actually have other plans.'

'Which are?' Jack had the cheek to ask.

'None of your business,' I said with spirit, adding, 'have a nice day,' and replaced the receiver before he could say another word.

The phone rang again almost immediately and I looked up to find Max watching me from the kitchen doorway. 'Aren't you going to answer it?' he looked at me quizzically.

'No. I think we can safely assume it will be a nuisance call and ignore it, but we obviously aren't going to get any peace here.'

'We could go to mine,' he suggested, with a definite glint in his eye, 'or we can go out to lunch, which is what I had planned in the first place — if you were free.'

I was tempted by the first suggestion, I

don't think Max could even begin to realize just how much I was tempted to just throw caution to the wind and go home with him, but it had been a very long time for me and I still didn't know him that well. Anyway, if he thought anything of me at all, he wouldn't mind waiting, I thought.

'Lunch, please,' I told him with a hint of apology in my tone, 'but I would love to see your place some other time. Do I need to change?'

He looked disappointed, but accepted my decision with good grace, and said, 'Lunch it is, then, and you don't need to change a thing.'

The phone, which had stopped ringing, started up again at that point and, snatching up a lightweight jacket I said, 'Let's go, shall we?'

It was only our third real date, by my reckoning, but there had been a subtle change in Max's manner towards me. He was much more tactile, holding my hand even for the short walk to the car, standing with his arm around my waist as we waited to be seated in the restaurant, and he deferred to me constantly, ensuring that everything was to my taste.

It felt as if we were taking our first steps towards a real relationship, but I accepted I could have been very wide of the mark and he might simply see me as a challenge. I was well aware I wasn't his usual choice of escort — I was probably a lot older for a start — and I really had no idea what on earth he might see in me or indeed what he had in mind for me.

It was almost a relief when he went to pay the bill, and left me for a few minutes with my thoughts.

I took a sip of wine and looked up to see him making his way back to me and I smiled at him across the room. There was no doubt in my mind that he was the most attractive man in the place and I could see I wasn't the only woman who thought so. It would be, oh, so easy to fall in love with him and I had to remind myself, quite firmly, that I actually hardly knew him or anything much about him and that he knew very little about me. So far, we had both been on our best behaviour.

'I missed you,' he said, sitting down and reaching for my hand across the table. 'Did you miss me?'

I laughed, 'Why would I, Max? I could see you across the room the whole time.'

He shook his head reprovingly and said, without a flicker of a smile, 'Sometimes I think this relationship is a tad onesided.'

'Why would you think that?' I was genuinely puzzled.

'Because I could be with you every minute of every day, make you my priority, but I'm not sure that I'm yours.'

'I have a family. You knew that before you started seeing me — and you *have* only just started seeing me, Max.'

'You have a grown-up son and I do accept that, and that we have only been seeing each other a short time. But you must know how I feel about you, Jo.'

'That's the thing, Max,' I said slowly, 'I don't.'

He looked surprised. 'I thought you must have realized,' he lifted my hand to his lips and kissed my fingertips one by one, never taking his gaze from my face. 'I'm falling in love with you and I want you so much the wait is killing me.'

How could I resist? I think we both knew he would be coming in with me when we got home and the tension in the car as he drove was palpable. I wasn't quite sure how we were even going to wait until we got inside. Swerving into a parking place, he braked sharply, scattering gravel and skidding to a halt. For a moment there was silence in the car, and then I think we both jumped at the sharp rap on the window next to me.

'Lizzie.' I stared through the glass and,

releasing the door, I jumped out and just about caught her as she fell weeping into my arms. 'Lizzie, my love, what on earth's wrong, sweetheart?'

# 21

Hiccoughing and crying, arms protectively round her baby bump, Lizzie did her best to tell me what was wrong.

'You'd best come inside. I'll make you a nice cup of tea and you can tell me all about it.'

Nodding, Lizzie allowed herself to be coaxed towards the communal front door. There was a dry cough behind us and we both turned to find Max standing there, his expression unreadable.

'I'll leave you to it, shall I?' he said, and I could only reply, 'I think that would be best,' and watch him drive away before ushering Lizzie inside and towards the stairs. I noticed he didn't look back.

We had only made it to the first step, when Greg came round the bend, all dressed up and evidently on his way out.

It must have been obvious that we were struggling and he offered immediately, 'Anything I can do to help?'

'If you could just help me to get Lizzie up the stairs that would be great and we shall be fine. Won't we, love? She's just a bit upset,' I offered by way of explanation.

'Sorry,' she murmured, and promptly burst into tears again.

'It's no trouble,' Greg assured her kindly, and taking an arm each we reached my flat in no time and got Lizzie settled comfortably.

'Thank you so much, Greg. We'll be OK now. You must get along or you'll make yourself late.' I didn't ask where he was going, feeling that was the least of my problems.

'It can wait while I put the kettle on. You stay with Lizzie.'

When I finally got to the bottom of it, the problem was, of course, Jack. I thought I might have known.

'We were getting on so well,' Lizzie sobbed, mopping at eyes that were already red and swollen, 'Pete and me, even thinking of moving in together before the baby was born and then — '

She cried even harder, and Greg came in carrying the tea tray and, looking at me over her head, raised his eyebrows in a silent query. I could only shrug in response.

I found a box of fresh tissues and dried her eyes again while Greg poured the tea, adding extra sugar to Lizzie's cup and advising her to, 'Take a sip, my love, it might help, we might be able to help.'

I was grateful for the 'we' because I felt less

alone with what I felt was going to be a huge problem, especially if Jack had anything to do with it. How I could have contemplated — even for the briefest moment — resuming a relationship that had been dead in the water for years was suddenly beyond me.

'I was happy that Pete was spending time with his Dad,' Lizzie seemed to have regained a somewhat precarious hold on her emotions and spoke more calmly, 'but I could tell Jack didn't like me and he's been busy trying to convince Pete that he has his whole life in front of him and shouldn't be getting tied down at his age.'

I was incensed. 'At his age! Doesn't he realize Petie isn't a boy any more, and that Petie isn't him? Jack was much older than Petie is now when he walked out on us, so age has nothing to do with it. Surely, Petie has more sense than to be swayed by that kind of talk?'

'I don't know,' Lizzie shook her head. 'He really does seem to be having second thoughts.'

I could quite happily have killed Jack at that point and I was more disappointed than I could say with Petie's behaviour. I'd really convinced myself over recent years that he had grown up and learned how to take responsibility. I would hate to find myself proved wrong.

'He'll come around,' I said in what I hoped was a convincing tone.

'I'm sure he will,' Greg put in firmly from where he'd been sitting quietly in charge of the teapot.

'You should go, Greg. We shouldn't have kept you. You're going to be late and we'll be fine now,' I insisted.

'Well, if you're sure.' He stood up, and Lizzie stood up, too, saying, 'I must go. I'm sure you have more important things to do than listen to me grizzling.'

'Nothing is more important to me at this moment,' I was saying as I also rose to my feet, 'than you and my grandchild. You must stay as long as you — '

Suddenly we were all staring in fascinated horror as a spreading pool of liquid formed on the carpet beneath Lizzie's feet.

'Oh, my God,' she said, grabbing at my arm. 'I'm so sorry.'

'It's fine,' I said, 'it's absolutely fine.'

'Would someone mind telling me what on earth is going on?' Greg was clearly mystified, and the look on his face lightened the moment, so that Lizzie and I both giggled.

'Her water's have ruptured,' I explained. 'The baby is on the way.'

'I have been having niggling pains for most of the day,' Lizzie confessed, 'but I just thought it was those Brackston Hicks or whatever they're called.'

'Should we be boiling kettles or something?' Greg looked ready to roll his sleeves up and get stuck in.

'Hardly,' I grinned, 'but we might need a lift to the hospital. You were going out, though.'

'Nothing that can't wait,' he was quick to assure me. 'What can I do now?'

The answer to that was provided by Lizzie herself, who suddenly bent double, gave an almighty groan, 'Ooomph, I think it's coming.'

Everything seemed to be happening so fast, and I had only limited experience to go on about how long a labour might take, but we managed to get Lizzie back down the stairs again.

Edna was fluttering, twittering and almost beside herself on the landing, and I managed to pass on Petie's mobile number and the name of the hospital with instructions to ring him *immediately*. When she called over the banister that she would ring the hospital also to let them know we were on our way I would have kissed her had she been closer.

'He won't come,' Lizzie said sadly, and then clutched her swollen belly as another contraction made her groan.

'He *will*,' I insisted, crossing my fingers behind her back.

Poor Greg. He must have been horrified at the thought of a baby being born in the back of his car, but you would never have known it. He saw us safely ensconced on the back seat before climbing into the driver's seat and advising us both to, 'Hold tight.'

Every traffic light was, predictably, red, cars pulled out in front of us and a removal lorry blocked the road for what felt like an eternity, and throughout the fraught journey Greg was calm and assured, telling us over and over, it would just be a few more minutes.

Everything seemed to happen at once when we reached the hospital. In the rush, it was assumed that I was Lizzie's mother and Greg was her father and none of us put them right. Lizzie was whipped away and I found myself in the delivery room with her so fast that my head was spinning.

'Where's Pete?' cried Lizzie, sweating and groaning.

'He'll be here any moment,' I assured her, and couldn't even cross my fingers because she had hold of my hands and was squeezing so tight all the feeling had long since gone.

'Is that the baby's father?' the midwife

asked from her vantage point at the foot of the bed and when I nodded, she assured Lizzie, 'They'll send him right in when he gets here. He's probably on his way right now.'

I mopped Lizzie's brow, told her she was doing a great job, and prayed for all I was worth that my son wouldn't let her down. I knew if he did I would find it very difficult to find it in my heart to forgive him.

Lizzie was pushing for all she was worth and the baby's head was crowning when Petie suddenly burst into the room, and he rushed to Lizzie's side. I said a silent prayer of thanks and let him take over, watching him kiss her sweetly, and whisper words of encouragement as their son came into the world — at which point we all promptly burst into tears.

Of course, we had no camera between us, which was something I bitterly regretted, because the two of them together cradling their baby would have made a marvellous picture.

I was so pleased I had mentioned it when Petie handed me his mobile phone and showed me how to take a photograph with that.

'And I'll take one of him with his Grandma,' he said and I found myself cradling the child who was going to make the biggest and best change to my life yet.

'His Grandpa, is he coming?' I looked towards the door as if I was expecting Jack to walk in, and part of me really was. I was quite sure he wouldn't want to miss out on such a great family occasion.

Petie threw me a frowning look and, shaking his head behind Lizzie's back, he mouthed, 'Later,' at me.

Lizzie obviously wasn't stupid and she hadn't missed a thing, despite appearing absorbed in her new baby. She smiled up at Petie and told him, 'I won't mind a bit if you want to invite him in. He is your dad.'

'He's not here and he won't be coming, either. He has no place in this family, he doesn't even know the meaning of the word, and I only wish I had realized that sooner.' He pointed at me and said, 'That's my mum *and* my dad standing right there — and what you call a *real* parent.'

Nothing more was said, as a tray of tea was kindly provided by the staff, and we enjoyed being what we were — a family. It was only later when both the baby and Lizzie slept that Petie gave me a whispered account of events.

At first, he said, he had accepted everything Jack said at face value, was simply excited to have him back in his life and had allowed Jack to all but convince him that us all becoming a family again was not only a possibility but a probability.

He had only found himself questioning the validity of this when he thought about the way I had taken control of my life these past weeks and how happy I had been. Then he started wondering if turning back the clock could seriously be what I wanted.

In fact, Petie had begun to realize, he told me, that it all seemed to be about what Jack wanted. Yet, as Petie said, *Jack* had walked out on us, *Jack* had instigated the divorce and had, apparently, been living his life quite happily without us for many years. So why the sudden change of heart?

'And if he so regretted leaving you and me, why was he so keen to encourage me to do the same to Lizzie and the baby?' Petie asked, 'Why was it only you and me he was interested in? Why the sudden determination to patch up a marriage he had thrown away without a second thought?'

'And did you find out?' I asked.

'I did,' he told me grimly, 'and the truth is not very flattering to either of us.'

'Tell me,' I insisted. 'I can assure you that nothing you tell me about Jack will surprise me.'

'Not even the fact he wanted us in his life

only so that he could meet the terms of his parents' will. It seems he never told them you two were divorced, and since they lived in Australia and never visited they weren't likely to find out, but they couldn't have entirely trusted him because the money was only left to him *provided his marriage to you was intact*.

'He'd been working on convincing the solicitor involved that we were a family by using photos taken when we were out together.' Petie shook his head in mock admiration. 'You have to hand it to him, he's one devious old bastard and obviously thought I was no better, because when I insisted on the truth, he actually thought I would go along with his bloody plan for a cut of the money.'

Petie kissed the sleeping baby's head and said sweetly, 'Excuse my language, my son, but I promise you will never, ever hear me speak like that again. I'm going to be a good dad, the best, just like my mum.'

I was still mopping my eyes when I left Petie, Lizzie and my brand new grandson together. Looking back at the perfect little family I was quite sure they would be, I silently wished them so much happiness in their new life together.

Then I focused my attention onto how I was going to get home, and recalled seeing a telephone booth in the main reception area. It was dark outside now, and though I had no real idea of the time, I figured it was probably only a short time before dawn would be breaking.

Pushing open the door, I thought the dimly lit room was empty and then I made out the dark shape of someone who appeared to be sleeping soundly on the long seat set along one wall. Someone whose wife was experiencing a long, drawn-out labour, perhaps or a granddad banished from the labour room. I was about to creep across to use the phone when a closer look revealed that the sleeping figure was no other than Greg. He must have been there for hours, waiting for news, and to make sure I got home safely.

I sat next to him for a moment, just watching him sleep and thinking what a kind and lovely man he was. A real family man, even though he had no children of his own. I knew without a doubt he would never have deserted his wife — or his child if he'd had one — as Jack had done without a thought, and neither would he have deprived his wife of her right to have a child as Max had tried to do. I could still recall the look on Max's face as he drove away rather than become involved in anything to do with my real life. I knew I had accepted in that moment that he could never be the man for me.

Just then, Greg opened his eyes, and as we stared at each other I realized that in just a few hours everything had changed — I had changed — and this time it had nothing to do with my appearance.

'Are you a grandmother?' he asked, sitting up in a hurry, and nodding, obviously delighted for me when I told him that I had a beautiful grandson.

*'It will be with someone you know but are not yet sure of.'* Those words suddenly had a whole new meaning and I wondered if it were possible the truth had been staring me in the face all along.

Then I remembered where Greg had been going when we had met him on the stairs all those hours ago. It forced me to come to my senses and realize that because I might have belatedly decided he was the man for me it didn't mean he was looking at me in the same way.

'You've been here for hours,' I said, 'and I'm so grateful to you for all your help, but I've ruined your evening with Gillian.'

He smiled at me then, the smile I had come to know and to love without even realizing it, and he said, 'Jo, I think we both know by now that it's not Gillian I want. I fell in love with you when I helped you write your list and decided there and then I wanted to be number one in your life if not on your list.'

'But why didn't you say anything?'

'I was waiting for you to realize you were already number one on mine.'

## THE END

We do hope that you have enjoyed reading this large print book.

Did you know that all of our titles are available for purchase?

We publish a wide range of high quality large print books including:
**Romances, Mysteries, Classics
General Fiction
Non Fiction and Westerns**

Special interest titles available in large print are:
**The Little Oxford Dictionary
Music Book
Song Book
Hymn Book
Service Book**

Also available from us courtesy of Oxford University Press:
**Young Readers' Dictionary
(large print edition)
Young Readers' Thesaurus
(large print edition)**

For further information or a free brochure, please contact us at:
**Ulverscroft Large Print Books Ltd.,
The Green, Bradgate Road, Anstey,
Leicester, LE7 7FU, England.
Tel:** (00 44) 0116 236 4325
**Fax:** (00 44) 0116 234 0205

*Other titles published by*
*The House of Ulverscroft:*

## SECOND BEST

**Pamela Fudge**

Stacey Trent has almost given up on love
when a whirlwind romance with Nick
Cable persuades her otherwise. Believing
they are to be married she turns her back
on home, career and friends to be with
him — only to discover that the promise of
a future together is just a tissue of lies.
Stacey is left to the mercy of his older
brother, Lex, but he's had enough of
clearing up Nick's trail of 'weeping
females'. However, circumstances force
them together, and an attraction grows
between them. But will Stacey convince
Lex he is more than second best?

# A BLESSING IN DISGUISE

## Pamela Fudge

When Alex Siddons becomes pregnant after twenty-five years of childless marriage, her life is turned upside down and her relationship with her husband, Phil, hangs in the balance. A child at their time of life is the last thing either of them wants or needs and yet, despite pressure from Phil, Alex cannot bring herself to terminate the pregnancy, even if it is the only thing that will save her marriage. Facing the prospect of life as a single mother, Alex finds unexpected support from within the Siddons family. Now she finally learns the true meaning of family and love.

# HIGH INFIDELITY

## Pamela Fudge

When a brief affair in Tina Brown's past resulted in an unplanned pregnancy, the decision was made not to share the news with the father, Calum Stacey. Tina raised the child alone, having decided to provide her with the full facts when she is eighteen years old. With her birthday just months away, Leanne is rushed into hospital with suspected meningitis and Tina feels she has no choice but to contact Calum without delay. Calum's engagement to a famous celebrity makes him newsworthy and there is mounting speculation surrounding his past. Can Tina and Calum protect their daughter from sudden media intrusion?

# WIDOW ON THE WORLD

## Pamela Fudge

Widowed at 46, Denise has come to the end of that first year alone and survived. It's time to get back out in the world and live her life. However, life — and her own family — seem to have other ideas, as her mother and daughter move into a house now bursting at the seams. A battle of wills ensues which Denise is determined to win, because only when she has sorted everyone else's lives out can she get on with her own. Romance doesn't figure in her calculations — but Denise should know that life doesn't always go according to plan . . .